SIDEWAYS STORIES FROM
WAYSIDE SCHOOL

THORNDIKE PRESS
A part of Gale, a Cengage Company

SIDEWAYS STORIES FROM
WAYSIDE SCHOOL

LOUIS SACHAR

ILLUSTRATED BY TIM HEITZ

GALE
A Cengage Company

LIBRARY OF CONGRESS CIP DATA ON FILE.
CATALOGUING IN PUBLICATION FOR THIS BOOK
IS AVAILABLE FROM THE LIBRARY OF CONGRESS.

ISBN-13: 978-1-4328-8127-6 (hardcover alk. paper)

Published in 2020 by arrangement with HarperCollins Children's Books, a division of HarperCollins Publishers.

Printed in Mexico
Print Number: 01   Print Year: 2020

*In memory of Robert J. Sachar
and to my mother, Andy, and Jeff.*

TABLE OF CONTENTS

INTRODUCTION

This book contains thirty stories about the children and teachers at Wayside School. But before we get to them, there is something you ought to know so that you don't get confused.

Wayside School was accidentally built sideways.

It was supposed to be only one story high, with thirty classrooms all in a row. Instead it is thirty stories high, with one classroom on each story. The builder said he was very sorry.

The children at Wayside like having a sideways school. They have an extra-large playground.

The children and teachers described in this book all go to class on the top floor. So there are thirty stories from the thirtieth story of Wayside School.

It has been said that these stories are strange and silly. That is probably true. However, when I told stories about you to the children at Wayside, they thought you were strange and silly. That is probably also true.

1
MRS. GORF

Mrs. Gorf had a long tongue and pointed ears. She was the meanest teacher in Wayside School. She taught the class on the thirtieth story.

"If you children are bad," she warned, "or if you answer a problem wrong, I'll wiggle my ears, stick out my tongue, and turn you into apples!" Mrs. Gorf didn't like children, but she loved apples.

Joe couldn't add. He couldn't even count. But he knew that if he answered a problem wrong, he would be turned into an apple. So he copied from John. He didn't like to cheat, but Mrs. Gorf had never taught him how to add.

One day Mrs. Gorf caught Joe copying John's paper.

She wiggled her ears — first her right one, then her left — stuck out her tongue, and turned Joe into an apple. Then she turned John into an apple for letting Joe cheat.

"Hey, that isn't fair," said Todd. "John was only trying to help a friend."

Mrs. Gorf wiggled her ears — first her right one, then her left — stuck out her tongue, and turned Todd into an apple.

"Does anybody else have an opinion?" she asked.

Nobody said a word.

Mrs. Gorf laughed and placed the three apples on her desk.

Stephen started to cry. He couldn't help it. He was scared.

"I do not allow crying in the classroom," said Mrs. Gorf. She wiggled her ears — first her right one, then her left — stuck out her tongue, and turned Stephen into an apple.

For the rest of the day, the children were absolutely quiet. And when they went home, they were too scared even to talk to their parents.

But Joe, John, Todd, and Stephen couldn't go home. Mrs. Gorf just left them on her desk. They were able to talk to each other, but they didn't have much to say.

Their parents were very worried. They didn't know where their children were. Nobody seemed to know.

The next day Kathy was late for school. As soon as she walked in, Mrs. Gorf turned her into an apple.

Paul sneezed during class. He was turned into an apple.

Nancy said, "God bless you!" when Paul sneezed. Mrs. Gorf wiggled her ears — first her right one, then her left — stuck out her tongue, and turned Nancy into an apple.

Terrence fell out of his chair. He was turned into an apple.

Maurecia tried to run away. She was halfway to the door as Mrs. Gorf's right ear began to wiggle. When she reached the door, Mrs. Gorf's left ear wiggled. Maurecia opened the door and had one foot

14

outside when Mrs. Gorf stuck out her tongue. Maurecia became an apple.

Mrs. Gorf picked up the apple from the floor and put it on her desk with the others. Then a funny thing happened. Mrs. Gorf turned around and fell over a piece of chalk.

The three Erics laughed. They were turned into apples.

Mrs. Gorf had a dozen apples on her desk: Joe, John, Todd, Stephen, Kathy, Paul, Nancy, Terrence, Maurecia, and the three Erics — Eric Fry, Eric Bacon, and Eric Ovens.

Louis, the yard teacher, walked into the classroom. He had missed the children at recess. He had heard that Mrs. Gorf was a mean teacher. So he came up to investigate. He saw the twelve apples on Mrs. Gorf's desk. "I must be wrong," he thought. "She must be a good teacher if so many children bring her apples." He walked back down to the playground.

The next day a dozen more children were turned into apples. Louis, the yard teacher, came back into the room. He saw twenty-four apples on Mrs. Gorf's desk. There were only three children left in the class. "She must be the best teacher in the world," he thought.

By the end of the week all of the children were apples. Mrs. Gorf was very happy. "Now I can go home," she said. "I don't have to teach anymore. I won't have to walk up thirty flights of stairs ever again."

"You're not going anywhere," shouted Todd. He jumped off the desk and bopped Mrs. Gorf on the nose. The rest of the apples followed. Mrs. Gorf fell on the floor. The apples jumped all over her.

16

"Stop," she shouted, "or I'll turn you into applesauce!"

But the apples didn't stop, and Mrs. Gorf could do nothing about it.

"Turn us back into children," Todd demanded.

Mrs. Gorf had no choice. She stuck out her tongue, wiggled her ears — this time her left one first, then her right — and turned the apples back into children.

"All right," said Maurecia, "let's go get Louis. He'll know what to do."

"No!" screamed Mrs. Gorf. "I'll turn you back into apples." She wiggled her ears — first her right one, then her left — and stuck out her tongue. But Jenny held up a mirror, and Mrs. Gorf turned herself into an apple.

The children didn't know what to do. They didn't have a teacher. Even though

Mrs. Gorf was mean, they didn't think it was right to leave her as an apple. But none of them knew how to wiggle their ears.

Louis, the yard teacher, walked in. "Where's Mrs. Gorf?" he asked.

Nobody said a word.

"Boy, am I hungry," said Louis. "I don't think Mrs. Gorf would mind if I ate this apple. After all, she always has so many."

He picked up the apple, which was really Mrs. Gorf, shined it up on his shirt, and ate it.

2
MRS. JEWLS

Mrs. Jewls had a terribly nice face. She stood at the bottom of Wayside School and looked up. She was supposed to teach the class on the thirtieth story.

The children on the thirtieth story were scared. They had never told anybody what had happened to Mrs. Gorf. They hadn't had a teacher for three days. They were afraid of what their new teacher would be like. They had heard she'd be a terribly nice teacher. They had never had a nice teacher. They were terribly afraid of nice teachers.

Mrs. Jewls walked up the winding, creaking staircase to the thirtieth story. She was also afraid. She was afraid of the children. She had heard that they would be horribly cute children. She had never taught cute children. She was horribly afraid of cute children.

She opened the door to the classroom. She was terribly nice. The children could tell just by looking at her.

Mrs. Jewls looked at the children. They were horribly cute. In fact, they were much too cute to be children.

"I don't believe it," said Mrs. Jewls. "It's a room full of monkeys!"

The children looked at each other. They didn't see any monkeys.

"This is ridiculous," said Mrs. Jewls, "just ridiculous. I walked all the way up thirty flights of stairs for nothing but a class of monkeys. What do they think I am? I'm a teacher, not a zookeeper!"

The children looked at her. They didn't know what to say. Todd scratched his head.

"Oh, I'm sorry," said Mrs. Jewls. "Please don't get me wrong. I have nothing against monkeys. It is just that I was expecting children. I like monkeys. I really do. Why, I'm sure we can play all kinds of monkey games."

"What are you talking about?" asked Todd.

Mrs. Jewls nearly fell off her chair. "Well, what do you know, a talking monkey. Tomorrow I'll bring you a banana."

"My name is Todd," said Todd.

The children were flabbergasted. They all raised their hands.

"I'm sorry," said Mrs. Jewls, "but I don't have enough bananas for all of you. I didn't expect this. Next week I'll bring in a whole bushel."

"I don't want a banana," said Calvin. "I'm not a monkey."

"Would you like a peanut?" asked Mrs. Jewls. "I think I might have a bag of peanuts in my purse. Wait a second. Yes, here it is."

"Thanks," said Calvin. Calvin liked peanuts.

Allison stood up. "I'm not a monkey," she said. "I'm a girl. My name is Allison. And so is everybody else."

Mrs. Jewls was shocked. "Do you mean to tell me that every monkey in here is named Allison?"

"No," said Jenny. "She means we are all children. My name is Jenny."

"No," said Mrs. Jewls. "You're much too cute to be children."

Jason raised his hand.

"Yes," said Mrs. Jewls, "the chimpanzee in the red shirt."

"My name is Jason," said Jason, "and I'm not a chimpanzee."

"You're too small to be a gorilla," said Mrs. Jewls.

"I'm a boy," said Jason.

"You're not a monkey?" asked Mrs. Jewls.

"No," said Jason.

"And the rest of the class, they're not monkeys, either?" asked Mrs. Jewls.

"No," said Allison. "That is what we've been trying to tell you."

"Are you sure?" asked Mrs. Jewls.

"We'd know if we were monkeys, wouldn't we?" asked Calvin.

"I don't know," said Mrs. Jewls. "Do monkeys know that they are monkeys?"

"I don't know," said Allison. "I'm not a monkey."

"No, I suppose you're not," said Mrs. Jewls. "Okay, in that case, we have a lot of work to do — reading, writing, subtraction, addition, spelling. Everybody take out a piece of paper. We will have a test now."

Jason tapped Todd on the shoulder. He said, "Do you want to know something? I liked it better when she thought we were monkeys."

"I know," said Todd. "I guess now it means she won't bring me a banana."

"There will be no talking in class," said Mrs. Jewls. She wrote Todd's name on the blackboard under the word DISCIPLINE.

24

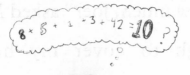

3
JOE

Joe had curly hair. But he didn't know how much hair he had. He couldn't count that high. In fact, he couldn't count at all.

When all of the other children went to recess, Mrs. Jewls told Joe to wait inside. "Joe," she said. "How much hair do you have?"

Joe shrugged his shoulders. "A lot," he answered.

"But how much, Joe?" asked Mrs. Jewls.

"Enough to cover my head," Joe answered.

"Joe, you are going to have to learn how to count," said Mrs. Jewls.

"But, Mrs. Jewls, I already know how to count," said Joe. "Let me go to recess."

"First count to ten," said Mrs. Jewls.

Joe counted to ten: "six, eight, twelve, one, five, two, seven, eleven, three, ten."

"No, Joe, that is wrong," said Mrs. Jewls.

"No, it isn't," said Joe. "I counted until I got to ten."

"But you were wrong," said Mrs. Jewls. "I'll prove it to you." She put five pencils on his desk. "How many pencils do we have here, Joe?"

Joe counted the pencils. "Four, six, one, nine, five. There are five pencils, Mrs. Jewls."

"That's wrong," said Mrs. Jewls.

"How many pencils are there?" Joe asked.

"Five," said Mrs. Jewls.

"That's what I said," said Joe. "May I go to recess now?"

"No," said Mrs. Jewls. "You got the right answer, but you counted the wrong way. You were just lucky." She set eight potatoes on his desk. "How many potatoes, Joe?"

Joe counted the potatoes. "Seven, five, three, one, two, four, six, eight. There are eight potatoes, Mrs. Jewls."

"No, there are eight," said Mrs. Jewls.

"But that's what I said," said Joe. "May I go to recess now?"

"No, you got the right answer, but you counted the wrong way again." She put three books on his desk. "Count the books, Joe."

Joe counted the books. "A thousand, a million, three. Three, Mrs. Jewls."

"Correct," said Mrs. Jewls.

"May I go to recess now?" Joe asked.

"No," said Mrs. Jewls.

"May I have a potato?" asked Joe.

"No. Listen to me. One, two, three, four, five, six, seven, eight, nine, ten," said Mrs. Jewls. "Now you say it."

"One, two, three, four, five, six, seven, eight, nine, ten," said Joe.

"Very good!" said Mrs. Jewls. She put six erasers on his desk. "Now count the erasers, Joe, just the way I showed you."

Joe counted the erasers. "One, two, three, four, five, six, seven, eight, nine, ten. There are ten, Mrs. Jewls."

"No," said Mrs. Jewls.

"Didn't I count right?" asked Joe.

"Yes, you counted right, but you got the wrong answer," said Mrs. Jewls.

"This doesn't make any sense," said Joe. "When I count the wrong way I get the right answer, and when I count right I get the wrong answer."

Mrs. Jewls hit her head against the wall five times. "How many times did I hit my head against the wall?" she asked.

"One, two, three, four, five, six, seven, eight, nine, ten. You hit your head against the wall ten times," said Joe.

"No," said Mrs. Jewls.

"Four, six, one, nine, five. You hit your head five times," said Joe.

Mrs. Jewls shook her head no and said, "Yes, that is right."

The bell rang, and all the other children came back from recess. The fresh air had made them very excited, and they were laughing and shouting.

"Oh, darn," said Joe. "Now I missed recess."

"Hey, Joe, where were you?" asked John. "You missed a great game of kickball."

"I kicked a home run," said Todd.

"What was wrong with you, Joe?" asked Joy.

"Nothing," said Joe. "Mrs. Jewls was just trying to teach me how to count."

Joy laughed. "You mean you don't know how to count!"

"Counting is easy," said Maurecia.

"Now, now," said Mrs. Jewls. "What's easy for you may not be easy for Joe, and what's easy for Joe may not be easy for you."

"Nothing's easy for Joe," said Maurecia. "He's stupid."

"I can beat you up," said Joe.

"Try it," said Maurecia.

"That will be enough of that," said Mrs. Jewls. She wrote Maurecia's name on the blackboard under the word DISCIPLINE.

Joe put his head on his desk between the eight potatoes and the six erasers.

"Don't feel bad, Joe," said Mrs. Jewls.

"I just don't get it," said Joe. "I'll never learn how to count."

"Sure you will, Joe," said Mrs. Jewls. "One day it will just come to you. You'll wake up one morning and suddenly be able to count."

Joe asked, "If all I have to do is wake up, what am I going to school for?"

"School just speeds things up," said Mrs. Jewls. "Without school it might take another seventy years before you wake up and are able to count."

"By that time I may have no hair left on top of my head to count," said Joe.

"Exactly," said Mrs. Jewls. "That is why you go to school."

When Joe woke up the next day, he knew how to count. He had fifty-five thousand and six hairs on his head. They were all curly.

4
SHARIE

Sharie had long eyelashes. She weighed only forty-nine pounds. She always wore a big red and blue overcoat with a hood. The overcoat weighed thirty-five pounds. The red part weighed fifteen pounds, the blue part weighed fifteen pounds, and the hood weighed five pounds. Her eyelashes weighed a pound and a half.

She sat next to the window in Mrs. Jewls's class. She spent a lot of time just staring out the window. Mrs. Jewls didn't mind. Mrs. Jewls said that a lot of people learn best when they stare out a window.

Sharie often fell asleep in class. Mrs. Jewls didn't mind that, either. She said that a lot of people do their best learning when they are asleep.

Sharie spent all of her time either looking out the window or sleeping. Mrs. Jewls thought she was the best student in the class.

One afternoon it was very hot. All of the windows were open, yet Sharie still wore her red and blue overcoat. The heat made her very tired. Mrs. Jewls was teaching arithmetic. Sharie pulled the hood up over her face, buried herself in the coat, and went to sleep.

"Mrs. Jewls," said Kathy, "Sharie is asleep."

"That's good," said Mrs. Jewls. "She must be learning something."

Mrs. Jewls continued with the lesson.

Sharie began to snore.

"Mrs. Jewls, Sharie is snoring," said Kathy.

"Yes, I can hear her," said Mrs. Jewls. "She must be learning an awful lot today. I wish the rest of you could be like her."

Sharie began to toss and turn. She flopped over on top of her desk, and then rolled over on top of Kathy's desk. Then she rolled back the other way. Kathy screamed. Sharie rolled out the window. She was still sound asleep.

As you know, Mrs. Jewls's class was on the thirtieth story of Wayside School. So Sharie had a long way to go.

After she had fallen ten stories, Sharie woke up. She looked around. She was confused. She wasn't in Mrs. Jewls's class, and she wasn't at home in bed. She couldn't figure out where she was. She yawned, pulled the hood back over her eyes, and went back to sleep. By that time she had fallen another ten stories.

Wayside School had an exceptionally large playground. Louis, the yard teacher, was way over on the other side of it when he happened to see Sharie fall out the window. He ducked under the volleyball net, hurtled past the kickball field, hopped over the hopscotch court, climbed through the monkey bars, sped across the grass, and caught Sharie just before she hit the ground.

The people in Mrs. Jewls's class cheered. Sharie woke up in Louis's arms.

"Darn it, Louis," she said. "What did you go and wake me up for?"

"I'm sorry, Sharie," said Louis.

"I'm sorry, I'm sorry," Sharie repeated. "Is that all you can say? I was having a wonderful dream until you woke me up. You're always bothering me, Louis. I can't stand it." She laughed and hugged him around the neck.

Louis carried her back up thirty flights of stairs to Mrs. Jewls's room.

That evening, when Sharie went to bed, she was unable to fall asleep. She just wasn't tired.

5
TODD

All of the children in Mrs. Jewls's class, except Todd, were talking and carrying on. Todd was thinking. Todd always thought before he spoke. When he got an idea, his eyes lit up.

Todd finished thinking and began to speak. But before he said two words, Mrs. Jewls called him.

"Todd," she said, "you know better than to talk in class. You must learn to work quietly, like the other children." She wrote his name on the blackboard under the word DISCIPLINE.

Todd looked around in amazement. All of the other children, who had been talking and screaming and fighting only seconds earlier, were quietly working in their workbooks. Todd scratched his head.

A child was given three chances in Mrs. Jewls's class. The first time he did something wrong, Mrs. Jewls wrote his name on the blackboard under the word DISCIPLINE. The second time he did something wrong, she put a check next to his name. And the third time he did something wrong, she circled his name.

Todd reached into his desk and pulled out his workbook. He had only just started on it when he felt someone tap him on the shoulder. It was Joy.

"What page are you on?" Joy asked.

"Page four," Todd whispered.

"I'm on page eleven," said Joy.

Todd didn't say anything. He didn't want to get into trouble. He just went back to work.

Five minutes later, Joy tapped him again. Todd ignored her. So Joy poked him in the back with her pencil. Todd pretended he didn't notice. Joy got up from her seat and sharpened her pencil. She came back and poked it in Todd's back. "What page are you on?" she asked.

"Page five," Todd answered.

"Boy, are you dumb," said Joy, "I'm on page twenty-nine."

"It isn't a race," Todd whispered.

Five minutes later Joy pulled Todd's hair and didn't let go until he turned around. "What page are you on?" she demanded.

"Page six," Todd answered as quietly as he could.

"I'M ON PAGE TWO HUNDRED!" Joy shouted.

Todd was very angry. "Will you please let me do my work and stop bothering me!"

Mrs. Jewls heard him. "Todd, what did I say about talking in class?"

Todd scratched his head.

Mrs. Jewls put a check next to Todd's name on the blackboard under the word DISCIPLINE.

Todd really tried to be good. He knew that if he talked one more time, Mrs. Jewls would circle his name. Then he'd have to go home early, at twelve o'clock, on the kindergarten bus, just as he had the day before and the day before that. In fact, there hadn't been a day since Mrs. Jewls took over the class that she didn't send Todd home early. She said she did it for his own good. The other children went home at two o'clock.

Todd wasn't really bad. He just always got caught. He really wanted to stay past twelve o'clock. He wanted to find out what the class did from twelve to two. But it didn't look as though this was going to be his day. It was only ten-thirty, and he already had two strikes against him. He sealed his lips and went back to work.

There was a knock on the door. Mrs. Jewls opened it. Two men stepped in wearing masks and holding guns. "Give us all your money!" they demanded.

"All I have is a nickel," said Mrs. Jewls.

42

"I have a dime," said Maurecia.

"I have thirteen cents," said Leslie.

"I have four cents," said Dameon.

"What kind of bank is this?" asked one of the robbers.

"It's not a bank, it's a school," said Todd. "Can't you read?"

"No," said the robbers.

"Neither can I," said Todd.

"Do you mean we walked all the way up thirty flights of stairs for nothing?" asked the robber. "Don't you have anything valuable?"

Todd's eyes lit up. "We sure do," he said. "We have knowledge." He grabbed Joy's workbook and gave it to the robbers. "Knowledge is much more valuable than money."

"Thanks, kid," said one of the robbers.

"Maybe I'll give up being a criminal and become a scientist," said the other.

They left the room without hurting anybody.

"Now I don't have a workbook," complained Joy.

Mrs. Jewls gave her a new one. Joy had to start all the way back at the beginning.

"Hey, Joy, what page are you on?" asked Todd.

"Page one," Joy sighed.

"I'm on page eight," laughed Todd triumphantly.

Mrs. Jewls heard him. She circled his name. Todd had three strikes against him. At twelve o'clock he left the room to go home early on the kindergarten bus.

But this time when he left, he was like a star baseball player leaving the field. All the children stood up, clapped their hands, and whistled.

Todd scratched his head.

6
BEBE

Bebe was a girl with short brown hair, a little beebee nose, totally tiny toes, and big brown eyes. Her full name was Bebe Gunn. She was the fastest draw in Mrs. Jewls's class.

She could draw a cat in less than forty-five seconds, a dog in less than thirty, and a flower in less than eight seconds.

But, of course, Bebe never drew just one dog, or one cat, or one flower. Art was from twelve-thirty to one-thirty. Why, in that time, she could draw fifty cats, a hundred flowers, twenty dogs, and several eggs or watermelons. It took her the same amount of time to draw a watermelon as an egg.

Calvin sat next to Bebe. He didn't think he was very good at art. Why, it took him the whole period just to draw one airplane. So instead, he just helped Bebe. He was Bebe's assistant. As soon as Bebe would finish one masterpiece, Calvin would take it from her and set down a clean sheet of paper. Whenever her crayon ran low, Calvin was ready with a new crayon. That way Bebe didn't have to waste any time. And in return, Bebe would draw five or six airplanes for Calvin.

It was twelve-thirty, time for art. Bebe was ready. On her desk was a sheet of yellow construction paper. In her hand was a green crayon.

Calvin was ready. He held a stack of paper and a box of crayons.

"Ready, Bebe," said Calvin.

"Ready, Calvin," said Bebe.

"Okay," said Mrs. Jewls, "time for art."

She had hardly finished her sentence when Bebe had already drawn a picture of a leaf.

Calvin took it from her and put another piece of paper down.

"Red," called Bebe.

Calvin handed Bebe a red crayon.

"Blue," called Bebe.

He gave her a blue crayon.

47

They were quite a pair. Their teamwork was remarkable. Bebe drew pictures as fast as Calvin could pick up the old paper and set down the new — a fish, an apple, three cherries, bing, bing, bing.

At one-thirty Mrs. Jewls announced, "Okay, class, art is over."

Bebe dropped her crayon and fell over on her desk. Calvin sighed and leaned back in his chair. He could hardly move. They had broken their old record. Bebe had drawn three hundred and seventy-eight pictures. They lay in a pile on Calvin's desk.

Mrs. Jewls walked by. "Calvin, did you draw all these pictures?"

Calvin laughed. "No, I can't draw. Bebe drew them all."

"Well, then, what did you draw?" asked Mrs. Jewls.

"I didn't draw anything," said Calvin.

"Why not? Don't you like art?" asked Mrs. Jewls.

"I love art," said Calvin. "That's why I didn't draw anything."

Mrs. Jewls did not understand.

"It would have taken me the whole period just to draw one picture," said Calvin. "And Bebe would only have been able to draw a hundred pictures. But with the two of us working together, she was able to draw three hundred and seventy-eight pictures! That's a lot more art."

Bebe and Calvin shook hands.

"No," said Mrs. Jewls. "That isn't how you measure art. It isn't how many pictures you have, but how good the pictures are. Why, a person could spend his whole life just drawing one picture of a cat. In that time I'm sure Bebe could draw a million cats."

"Two million," said Bebe.

Mrs. Jewls continued. "But if that one picture is better than each of Bebe's two million, then that person has produced more art than Bebe."

Bebe looked as if she was going to cry. She picked up all the pictures from Calvin's desk and threw them in the garbage. Then she ran from the room.

"I thought her pictures were good," said Calvin. He reached into the garbage pail and took out a crumpled-up picture of an airplane.

Bebe walked outside into the playground.

Louis, the yard teacher, spotted her. "Where are you going?" he asked.

"I'm going home to draw a picture of a cat," said Bebe.

"Will you bring it to school and show it to me tomorrow?" Louis asked.

"Tomorrow!" laughed Bebe. "By tomorrow I doubt if I'll even be finished with one whisker."

7
CALVIN

Calvin had a big, round face.

"Calvin," said Mrs. Jewls, "I want you to take this note to Miss Zarves for me."

"Miss Zarves?" asked Calvin.

"Yes, Miss Zarves," said Mrs. Jewls. "You know where she is, don't you?"

"Yes," said Calvin. "She's on the nine-teenth story."

"That's right, Calvin," said Mrs. Jewls. "Take it to her."

Calvin didn't move.

"Well, what are you waiting for?" asked Mrs. Jewls.

"She's on the nineteenth story," said Calvin.

"Yes, we have already established that fact," said Mrs. Jewls.

"The nineteenth story," Calvin repeated.

"Yes, Calvin, the nineteenth story," said Mrs. Jewls. "Now take it to her before I lose my patience."

"But, Mrs. Jewls," said Calvin.

"Now, Calvin!" said Mrs. Jewls. "Unless you would rather go home on the kinder-garten bus."

"Yes, ma'am," said Calvin. Slowly he walked out the door.

"Ha, ha, ha," laughed Terrence, "take it to the nineteenth story."

"Give it to Miss Zarves," hooted Myron.

"Have fun on the nineteenth story," called Jason.

Calvin stood outside the door to the classroom. He didn't know where to go.

As you know, when the builder built Wayside School, he accidentally built it sideways. But he also forgot to build the nineteenth story. He built the eighteenth and the twentieth, but no nineteenth. He said he was very sorry.

There was also no Miss Zarves. Miss Zarves taught the class on the nineteenth story. Since there was no nineteenth story, there was no Miss Zarves.

And besides that, as if Calvin didn't have enough problems, there was no note. Mrs. Jewls had never given Calvin the note.

"Boy, this is just great," thought Calvin. "Just great! I'm supposed to take a note that I don't have to a teacher who doesn't exist, and who teaches on a story that was never built."

He didn't know what to do. He walked down to the eighteenth story, then back up to the twentieth, then back down to the eighteenth, and back up again to the twentieth. There was no nineteenth story. There never was a nineteenth story. And there never will be a nineteenth story.

Calvin walked down to the administration office. He decided to put the note in Miss Zarves's mailbox. But there wasn't one of those, either. That didn't bother Calvin too much, however, since he didn't have a note.

He looked out the window and saw Louis, the yard teacher, shooting baskets. "Louis will know what to do," he thought. Calvin went outside.

"Hey, Louis," Calvin called.

"Hi, Calvin," said Louis. He tossed him the basketball. Calvin dribbled up and took a shot. He missed. Louis tipped it in.

"Do you want to play a game?" Louis asked.

"I don't have time," said Calvin. "I have to deliver a note to Miss Zarves up on the nineteenth story."

"Then what are you doing all the way down here?" Louis asked.

"There is no nineteenth story," said Calvin.

"Then where is Miss Zarves?" asked Louis.

"There is no Miss Zarves," said Calvin.

"What are you going to do with the note?" asked Louis.

"There is no note," said Calvin.

"I understand," said Louis.

"That's good," said Calvin, "because I sure don't."

"It's very simple," said Louis. "You are not supposed to take no notes to no teachers. You already haven't done it."

Calvin still didn't understand. "I'll just have to tell Mrs. Jewls that I couldn't deliver the note," he said.

"That's good," said Louis. "The truth is always best. Besides, I don't think I understand what I said, either." Calvin walked back up the thirty flights of stairs to Mrs. Jewls's class.

"Thank you very much, Calvin," said Mrs. Jewls.

Calvin said, "But I —"

Mrs. Jewls interrupted him. "That was a very important note, and I'm glad I was able to count on you."

"Yes, but you see —" said Calvin.

"You delivered the note to Miss Zarves on the nineteenth story?" asked Jason. "How did you do it?"

"What do you mean, how did he do it?" asked Mrs. Jewls. "He gave Miss Zarves the note. Some people, Jason, are responsible."

"But you see, Mrs. Jewls —" said Calvin.

"The note was very important," said Mrs. Jewls. "I told Miss Zarves not to meet me for lunch."

"Don't worry," said Calvin. "She won't."

"Good," said Mrs. Jewls. "I have a coffee can full of Tootsie Roll pops on my desk. You may help yourself to one, for being such a good messenger."

"Thanks," said Calvin, "but really, it was nothing."

8
MYRON

Myron had big ears. He was elected class president. The children in Mrs. Jewls's class expected him to be a good president. Other presidents were good speakers. Myron was even better. He was a good listener.

But he had a problem. He didn't know what a class president was supposed to do. So he asked.

"What am I supposed to do?"

"It's a difficult job," said Mrs. Jewls. "But you can do it. You must turn the lights on every morning and turn them off at the end of the day."

"What?" asked Myron.

"As a class president you must learn to listen," said Mrs. Jewls. "I'll repeat myself only one more time. You must turn the lights on every morning —"

"I heard you the first time," said Myron. "It just doesn't sound like much of a job."

"It certainly is!" said Mrs. Jewls. "Without light I can't teach, and the children can't learn. Only you can give us that light. I think it is a very important job."

"I guess so," said Myron. He wasn't convinced.

"Here, let me show you how to work a light switch," said Mrs. Jewls.

60

"I already know how," said Myron. "I've been turning lights on and off all my life."

"Very good!" said Mrs. Jewls. "You'll make a fine president."

Myron wanted to be the best president ever. But it was such an easy job, he thought, that anybody could do it. When school let out that day, Myron stayed behind. He turned out the lights by flicking the switch down.

"Excellent!" said Mrs. Jewls.

On his way home, Myron heard a horrible noise. First there was a loud screeching, then a sharp squeal, a roaring engine, and then the very faint sound of a girl crying.

Myron ran to see what had happened.

Dana was bent over in the middle of the road.

"What's the matter?" asked Myron.

"My dog, Pugsy, was hit by a car," Dana cried.

"Who did it?" asked Myron.

"I don't know!" Dana sobbed. "They sped away."

"Well, that's not important," said Myron. "We've got to try to save Pugsy."

Pugsy lay unconscious in the street. Myron carefully picked her up. He carried her two miles to the vet. Dana cried at his side.

"Don't worry, Dana," said Myron. "She'll be all right." But he wasn't really so sure.

He gave Pugsy to the vet, walked Dana home, then walked home himself.

Dana was so upset that she forgot to thank him. Myron didn't mind. He thought that was what being class president was all about.

The next morning, before he went to school, Myron went to Dana's house. Pugsy was there. She seemed all right.

Dana petted her. Pugsy licked her face.

"See, Myron, she's all right," said Dana. "The vet said that you brought her in just in time."

"Hi, Pugsy," said Myron. He petted her.

Pugsy bit his hand.

"I guess she doesn't know you," said Dana. "She was unconscious yesterday when you saved her life."

Dana's mother put some medicine and a Band-Aid on Myron's hand. Then she drove the children to school.

They were late. They ran up the stairs to Mrs. Jewls's class. The room was completely dark.

"It's about time you got here, Myron," said Mrs. Jewls. "We have no lights."

"Why didn't somebody else just turn them on?" asked Myron.

"Because you're class president," said Mrs. Jewls. "Show Stephen how to work the lights. From now on he will be class president."

Myron showed Stephen how to turn on the lights. He flicked the switch up.

At the end of the day, Myron showed Stephen how to turn the lights off. He flicked the switch down.

After a week, Stephen finally caught on. He made a good president. The lights were on every morning.

Myron, who was president for only a day, was the best president in the history of Wayside School. It was just that nobody knew it.

9
MAURECIA

Maurecia liked ice cream. She was sweet and pretty and could beat up any boy in Mrs. Jewls's class. Everybody liked Maurecia — except Kathy, but then she didn't like anybody. Maurecia only liked ice cream.

Every day Maurecia brought an ice cream cone to school and kept it in her desk until lunch time. At first she brought chocolate ice cream every day. But she soon tired of chocolate ice cream. So she started bringing vanilla. But she got tired of vanilla, too. Then she got tired of strawberry, fudge ripple, butter pecan, pistachio, and burgundy cherry, in that order. And then a terrible thing happened. Maurecia got tired of ice cream. By that time her desk was a mess, and everything in it was sticky.

Everybody liked Maurecia. But Maurecia didn't like anything.

Mrs. Jewls hated to see Maurecia unhappy.

"I don't understand it, Mrs. Jewls," cried Maurecia. "There just aren't any good flavors anymore."

So Mrs. Jewls worked all night. The next day she brought in a new flavor of ice cream for Maurecia. It was Maurecia-flavored ice cream. "Everybody will like it," thought Mrs. Jewls, "because everybody likes Maurecia."

"Here you are, Maurecia," said Mrs. Jewls, "Maurecia-flavored ice cream."

Everybody gathered around as Maurecia tasted it. They hoped she'd like it.

Maurecia took a lick.

"Well?" said Mrs. Jewls.

Maurecia took another lick.

"Well?" asked the class.

"This ice cream has no taste," said Maurecia. "It doesn't taste bad, but it doesn't taste good. It doesn't taste like anything at all!"

Mrs. Jewls was heartbroken.

"Here, let me try it," said Todd. He tasted it. "You're crazy, Maurecia!" he said. "This is the best-tasting ice cream I've ever eaten! Try some, Deedee."

"Ummmmmmmmmm, it's delicious," said Dee-dee. "It's so sweet and creamy." She passed it around the room.

"Oh, it is so good," said Leslie.

"I think it tastes terrible," said Kathy.

"I don't understand it," said Maurecia. "I don't taste a thing."

Mrs. Jewls slapped herself in the face. "Oh, I've made a big mistake, Maurecia. Of course you can't taste anything. It's Maurecia-flavored ice cream. It's the same taste you always taste when you're not tasting anything at all."

So the next day Mrs. Jewls brought in Joe-flavored ice cream. Maurecia liked it. So did everybody else. Joe thought it had no taste.

Everybody liked Maurecia. Maurecia only liked Joe.

The following day Mrs. Jewls brought in Ron-flavored ice cream. Ron thought it had no taste, but everybody else loved it.

Everybody liked Maurecia. Maurecia only liked Joe and Ron.

By the end of the month, Mrs. Jewls had brought in twenty-seven new flavors of ice cream, one for each member of the class.

Everybody liked Maurecia, and Maurecia liked everybody. They all tasted so good. All except Kathy, that is. Kathy-flavored ice cream tasted a little bit like old bologna.

Everyone still agreed that Maurecia-flavored ice cream was the best, except Maurecia. She liked Todd ice cream the best.

This turned out to be a problem. Every once in a while Maurecia would try to take a bite out of Todd's arm in order to get that very special flavor.

10
PAUL

Paul had the best seat in Mrs. Jewls's class. He sat in the back of the room. It was the seat that was the farthest away from Mrs. Jewls.

Mrs. Jewls was teaching the class about fractions. She drew a picture of a pie on the blackboard. She cut the pie into eight pieces. She explained that each piece was one-eighth of the pie.

Paul never paid attention. He didn't see the picture of the pie. He didn't see anything.

Well, he did see one thing.

Actually, he saw two things.

He saw Leslie's two pigtails.

Leslie sat in front of Paul. She had two long, brown pigtails that reached all the way down to her waist.

Paul saw those pigtails, and a terrible urge came over him. He wanted to pull a pigtail. He wanted to wrap his fist around it, feel the hair between his fingers, and just yank.

He thought it would also be fun to tie the pigtails together, or better yet, tie them to her chair. But most of all, he just wanted to pull one.

Slowly he reached for the one on the right. "NO! What am I doing?" he thought. "I'll only get into trouble."

Paul had it made. He sat in the back of the room. He paid no attention to anyone, and nobody paid any attention to him. But if he pulled a pigtail, it would be all over. Leslie would tell on him, and he'd become the center of attention.

He sighed and slowly withdrew his arm.

But Paul couldn't ignore those pigtails. There they were, dangling right in front of him, just begging to be pulled. He could close his eyes, but he couldn't make the pigtails disappear. He could still smell them. And hear them. He could almost taste them.

"Maybe just a little tug," he thought. "No, none."

There they hung, easily within his reach.

"Well let them just hang there!" thought Paul.

It would be foolish to pull one, no matter how tempting they were. None of the other children in the class pulled pigtails; why should he? Of course, none of the other children sat behind Leslie, either.

It was just a simple matter of being able to think clearly. That was all. Paul thought it over and decided not to pull one. It was as simple as that.

Suddenly his arm shot forward. He grabbed Leslie's right pigtail and yanked.

"Yaaaaaahhhhhhhhhh!" screamed Leslie.

Everybody looked at her.

"Paul pulled my pigtail," she said.

They all looked at Paul.

"I . . . I couldn't help it," said Paul.

"You'd better learn to help it," said Mrs. Jewls. She wrote Paul's name on the blackboard under the word DISCIPLINE. "Tell Leslie you're sorry."

"I'm sorry, Leslie," said Paul.

"Hmmmph," said Leslie.

Paul felt horrible. Never again would he pull another pigtail! Except, there was one problem. He still wasn't satisfied. He had pulled the right one, but that wasn't enough. He wanted to pull the left one, too. It was as if he heard a little voice coming from the pigtail saying, "Pull me, Paul. Pull me."

"I can't," Paul answered. "My name's already on the blackboard under the word DISCIPLINE."

"Big deal," said the pigtail. "Pull me."

"No way," said Paul. "Never again."

75

"Aw, come on, Paul, just a little tug," urged the pigtail. "What harm could it do?"

"Lots of harm," said Paul. "Leslie will scream, and I'll get in trouble again."

"Boy, that's not fair," whined the pigtail. "You pulled the right one. Now it's my turn."

"I know, but I can't," said Paul.

"Sure you can," said the pigtail. "Just grab me and yank."

"No," said Paul. "It's not right."

"Sure it is, Paul," said the pigtail. "Pigtails are meant to be pulled. That's what we're here for."

"Tell that to Leslie," said Paul.

"Leslie won't mind," said the pigtail. "I promise."

"I bet," said Paul. "Just like she didn't mind the last time."

"You just didn't pull hard enough," said the pigtail. "Leslie likes us pulled real hard."

"Really?" asked Paul.

"Cross my heart," said the pigtail, "the harder, the better."

"Okay," said Paul, "but if you're lying. . . ."

"I promise," said the pigtail.

Paul grabbed the left pigtail. It felt good in his hand. He pulled as hard as he could.

"Yaaaaaaaaaahhhhhhhhhhhhhhhhhhhhhh!!!" screamed Leslie.

Mrs. Jewls asked, "Paul, did you pull Leslie's pigtail again?"

"No," said Paul. "I pulled the other one."

All the children laughed.

"Are you trying to be funny?" asked Mrs. Jewls.

"No," said Paul. "I was trying to be fair. I couldn't pull one and not the other."

The children laughed again.

"Pigtails are meant to be pulled," Paul concluded.

Mrs. Jewls put a check next to Paul's name on the blackboard under the word DISCIPLINE.

But at last Paul was satisfied. True, his name was on the blackboard with a check next to it, but that really didn't matter. All he had to do was stay out of trouble the rest of the day, and his name would be erased. It's easy to stay out of trouble when you have the best seat in the class.

In fact, Paul could do this every day. He could pull Leslie's pigtails twice, and then stay out of trouble the rest of the day. There was nothing Leslie could do about it.

Suddenly, out of nowhere, Leslie screamed, "Yaaaahhhhhhhh!"

Mrs. Jewls circled Paul's name and sent him home early on the kindergarten bus. Nobody would believe that he hadn't pulled Leslie's pigtail again.

11
DANA

Dana had four beautiful eyes. She wore glasses. But her eyes were so beautiful that the glasses only made her prettier. With two eyes she was pretty. With four eyes she was beautiful. With six eyes she would have been even more beautiful. And if she had a hundred eyes, all over her face and her arms and her feet, why, she would have been the most beautiful creature in the world.

But poor Dana wasn't covered from head to foot with beautiful eyes. She was covered with mosquito bites.

Mrs. Jewls picked up her yardstick and said, "Now it's time for arithmetic."

"Oh, no, Mrs. Jewls," said Dana. "I can't do arithmetic. I itch all over. I can't concentrate."

"But we have all kinds of arithmetic," said Mrs. Jewls, "addition without carrying, addition with carrying, and carrying without addition."

"I don't care," cried Dana.

"We have that, too," said Mrs. Jewls, "addition without caring. Now, stop carrying on."

Dana whined, "I can't, Mrs. Jewls. I itch too much."

"And I'm too thirsty," said D.J.

"I'm too tired," said Ron.

"I'm too hungry," said Terrence.

"I'm too stupid," said Todd.

Mrs. Jewls hit her desk with her yardstick. Everyone stopped talking.

Mrs. Jewls said, "We are going to have arithmetic now, and I don't want to hear another thing about it."

"But, Mrs. Jewls, I really do itch. I can't do arithmetic," Dana whined.

"No," said Mrs. Jewls. "Arithmetic is the best known cure for an itch. How many mosquito bites do you have?"

"I don't know," said Dana, "over a hundred. First I try scratching one, but then another one starts to itch. So I scratch that one, and that one stops, and another one starts. So I scratch that one, and the itch moves down to another one. Then it goes back to the first one. The itch just never stays in the same place. I just can't scratch them all."

"What you need is a good, strong dose of arithmetic," said Mrs. Jewls.

"I'd rather have calamine lotion," said Dana.

"Remember, Dana," said Mrs. Jewls, "mosquito bites itch, not numbers."

"So what?" said Dana.

Mrs. Jewls continued. "We'll just have to turn your mosquito bites into numbers."

"I'm a mess," Dana moaned.

Mrs. Jewls began to turn the mosquito bites into numbers. "How much is three mosquito bites plus three mosquito bites?" she asked.

Rondi raised her hand. "Six mosquito bites," she answered.

"How much is six mosquito bites minus two mosquito bites?" asked Mrs. Jewls.

"Four mosquito bites," said D.J.

"How much is five mosquito bites times two?" asked Mrs. Jewls.

"Ten mosquito bites," said Bebe.

"Very good," said Mrs. Jewls.

"I still itch," Dana complained.

"I've got one more question," said Mrs. Jewls. "How much is forty-nine mosquito bites plus seventy-five mosquito bites?"

Nobody raised a hand.

"Think, class," said Mrs. Jewls. "This is for Dana."

Nobody knew the answer. Dana's itch began to get worse and worse.

At last, Dana began counting her own mosquito bites. She counted seventy-five on one side and forty-nine on the other.

Then she added them together for a total of one hundred and twenty-four mosquito bites.

"One hundred and twenty-four mosquito bites," Dana called.

"Very good," said Mrs. Jewls.

Dana had one hundred and twenty-four mosquito bites. And none of them itched anymore.

"I'm still thirsty," said D.J. "Can arithmetic do anything for that?"

"I'm still tired," said Ron.

"I'm still hungry," said Terrence.

"I'm still stupid," said Todd.

"I'm glad we turned my mosquito bites into numbers instead of letters," said Dana. "I could never spell *mosquito*."

12
JASON

Jason had a small face and a big mouth. He had the second biggest mouth in Mrs. Jewls's class. And there were an awful lot of big mouths in that class.

"Mrs. Jewls," Jason called without raising his hand. "Joy is chewing gum in class!"

Joy had the biggest mouth in Mrs. Jewls's class. And it was filled with gum. There was hardly even room for her tongue.

"Joy, I'm ashamed of you," said Mrs. Jewls. "I'm afraid I'll have to put your name up on the board."

"That's okay, Mrs. Jewls," Jason called. "I'll do it." Jason hopped out of his seat and wrote Joy's name on the blackboard under the word DISCIPLINE.

While he was up, Joy took the glob of gum out of her mouth and placed it on Jason's chair.

Rondi and Allison giggled.

Jason walked back from the blackboard to his desk and sat down. "Mrs. Jewls," he called, "I'm STUCK!"

Rondi and Allison giggled again.

Mrs. Jewls got angry. "Joy, you're going home on the kindergarten bus today."

"Oh, good," said Todd. "I'll have some company." Todd went home on the kindergarten bus every day. He could never seem to make it to twelve o'clock without getting into trouble three times. His name wasn't even up on the blackboard yet. But he knew that by twelve o'clock it would be up, checked, and circled.

"Mrs. Jewls, what am I going to do? I'm stuck! I'm going to have to stay here the rest of my life!" said Jason.

"Joy, tell Jason you're sorry," said Mrs. Jewls.

"I'm sorry, Jason," said Joy.

"Oh, that's okay, Joy," said Jason. "I don't mind."

"Try to get up, Jason," said Mrs. Jewls.

Jason tried. "I can't, Mrs. Jewls. I'm stuck."

Mrs. Jewls asked the three Erics to help. Eric Fry and Eric Ovens pulled Jason. Eric Bacon held the chair.

"Stop," cried Jason. "You'll rip my pants."

Rondi and Allison giggled.

"All right," said Mrs. Jewls. "Let's try ice water. That should freeze the gum and make it less sticky. I'll go get some from Miss Mush."

Miss Mush was the lunch teacher at Wayside School. She had the remarkable ability to undercook a dish and overcook it at the same time. Her specialty was a nice, hot bowl of mud. She called it porridge.

Jason looked at Rondi and Allison. "No, Mrs. Jewls," he said. "Don't leave me. Besides, Miss Mush's ice water is probably warm."

"Don't be silly, Jason," said Mrs. Jewls. "I'm sure it will be at least as cold as her soups."

Rondi and Allison leered at Jason.

"No, Mrs. Jewls, don't go!" begged Jason.

"I'll be right back, Jason," said Mrs. Jewls. She went to Miss Mush for some ice water.

As soon as Mrs. Jewls stepped out the door, Rondi and Allison jumped up from their seats and started to tickle Jason. He laughed until his hair turned purple. The girls got back to their seats just as Mrs. Jewls returned.

Mrs. Jewls carried a big bucket of ice cold water.

"Oh, no, please don't, no!" Jason pleaded.

"We have no choice," said Mrs. Jewls. She threw the water all over him.

"Well," said Mrs. Jewls, "try to get up."

Jason was drenched. "I'm wet and I'm cold and I'm still stuck!"

"Oh, well, it didn't work," said Mrs. Jewls. "At least we tried. Now I guess we'll have to cut your pants off."

Rondi and Allison giggled.

"No, Mrs. Jewls, no!" Jason screamed. "I don't mind being stuck here. I'm really very comfortable."

"Don't be silly, Jason," said Mrs. Jewls.

"Don't cut off my pants," said Jason.

"The three Erics can carry you to the bathroom," said Mrs. Jewls. "I'll ask Louis to call your mother. She can bring you a new pair of pants."

The three Erics took hold of Jason's chair and turned him upside down.

"No, Mrs. Jewls," said Jason. "Now I'll always have a place to sit down. I won't have to worry about finding a seat on the bus."

The three Erics began to take him away.

"Wait," said Joy. "Mrs. Jewls, if I can get Jason unstuck, do I still have to go home on the kindergarten bus?"

"All right," said Mrs. Jewls. "If you can somehow get Jason free, you don't have to go home early."

"Don't trust her, Mrs. Jewls," said Jason. He was still hanging upside down.

"I'll just kiss him," said Joy.

"No!" Jason screamed. "Don't let her kiss me, Mrs. Jewls. Throw water on me. Tickle me. Cut off my pants. Hang me upside down from the ceiling. But don't let her kiss me!"

"I'll just kiss him on the nose," said Joy.

"We've got nothing to lose, Jason," said Mrs. Jewls.

"Oooooh, who would want to kiss Jason!" said Allison.

Jason hung helplessly upside down.

Joy stepped up and kissed him on the nose.

Jason fell out of the chair and hit his head on the floor.

Rondi and Allison giggled.

"Darn," said Todd. "Now I'll have to go home alone again."

Joy erased her name from the blackboard.

13
RONDI

Rondi had twenty-two beautiful teeth. Everyone else had twenty-four. Rondi was missing her two front teeth. And those were the most beautiful teeth of all.

"Your front teeth are so cute," said Mrs. Jewls. "They make you look just adorable."

"But, Mrs. Jewls," said Rondi. "I don't have any front teeth."

"I know," said Mrs. Jewls. "That's what makes them so cute."

Rondi didn't understand.

"'Oooh, Rondi, I just love your two front teeth," said Maurecia. "I wish I had some like that."

"But I don't have them," said Rondi.

"That's why I love them so much," said Maurecia.

"Oh, this is silly," said Rondi. "Everybody thinks the teeth I don't have are cute. I'm not wearing a coat. Don't you all just love my coat? And what about my third arm? I don't have one. Isn't it lovely?"

"Love your hat, Rondi," said Joy.

"I'm not wearing a hat!" Rondi screamed.

"That's what makes it so interesting," said Joy. "Don't you think so, Leslie?"

"Oh, yes," said Leslie. "It's a very nice hat. Nice boots, too."

"I'm not wearing boots!" Rondi insisted.

"Yes," said Joy, "very nice boots. They go so well with your hat."

"What hat?" asked Rondi.

"Yes," Leslie agreed. "Rondi showed excellent taste by not wearing the hat or the boots. They go so well together."

Rondi had had enough. She covered her head so nobody could see her hat. She put her feet under her desk so nobody could see her boots. Then she closed her mouth tightly so nobody could see her two front teeth.

Suddenly, everybody who was sitting near her began to laugh.

"What's so funny?" asked Todd.

96

"The joke Rondi didn't tell," said Jason.

"Ask Rondi not to tell it again, Todd," said Calvin.

"Rondi," said Todd, "don't tell it again."

Rondi was horrified. She didn't know what to do. She kept her mouth shut and just stared at Todd. To her amazement, Todd laughed.

"Hey, everybody," called Todd. "Listen to Rondi's joke."

Rondi didn't say a word, but the rest of the class began to laugh.

Mrs. Jewls got very angry. She wrote Rondi's name on the blackboard under the word DISCIPLINE.

"The classroom is not the place for jokes," she said.

"But, Mrs. Jewls," said Rondi. "I didn't tell a joke."

"Yes, I know," said Mrs. Jewls, "but the funniest jokes are the ones that remain untold."

"Okay, okay," said Rondi. "If that's what you want, then that's what you'll get. I'll really tell a joke. That way I won't disturb the class. And tomorrow I'll wear boots and a hat. Of course, you won't like them as much as the ones I didn't wear today. But I better hurry up and tell my joke before you all start to laugh.

"There was a monkey sitting in a banana tree. He was very hungry. He knew that somewhere in the tree there was a magic banana, and that once he ate that banana, he wouldn't be hungry anymore. He ate one banana. That wasn't it. He was still hungry. He ate another banana. That one wasn't it, either. He was still hungry. Finally, after he ate his tenth banana, he wasn't hungry anymore. 'I knew I'd find it,' he said. 'It's too bad I didn't eat that one first. I wouldn't have had to waste all those other bananas.'"

Nobody laughed. Nobody had even listened to Rondi. Mrs. Jewls was busy teaching arithmetic, and everybody else was paying strict attention.

Rondi slapped herself in the face to make sure she was really there. She was.

The bell rang for recess. Rondi ran outside. She was very upset.

Louis, the yard teacher, saw her. "Why the frown, Rondi?" he asked. "Come on, smile. Let me see your cute front teeth."

Rondi screamed. She socked Louis in the stomach, then bit his arm with her missing teeth. And that kind of bite hurts the worst.

14
SAMMY

It was a horrible, stinky, rainy day. Some rainy days are fun and exciting, but not this one. This one stunk. All the children were wet and wore smelly raincoats. The whole room smelled awful.

"Ooooh, it stinks in here," said Maurecia. Everybody laughed. But she was right.

There was one good thing, however. There was a new boy in class. New kids are always fun. Except no one could even tell what the new boy looked like. He was completely covered by his raincoat.

"Class," said Mrs. Jewls. "I'd like you all to meet Sammy. Let us show him what a nice class we can be."

Leslie walked up and smiled at Sammy. But her smile quickly turned into a frown. "You smell terrible," she said.

"Leslie!" exclaimed Mrs. Jewls. "That's no way to greet a new member of our class." Mrs. Jewls wrote Leslie's name on the blackboard under the word DISCIPLINE.

"But he does, Mrs. Jewls," said Leslie. "He smells awful."

"You're ugly," Sammy replied.

"Now, Sammy, that's no way to talk," said Mrs. Jewls. "Leslie's a very pretty girl."

"She's ugly," said Sammy.

Allison spoke up. "Well, you smell terrible and are probably even uglier. But nobody can see you because you are hiding under that smelly old raincoat."

"That will be enough of that," said Mrs. Jewls. "Now, Sammy, why don't you take off your coat and hang it in the closet? Let us all see how nice you look."

"I don't want to, you old windbag," said Sammy.

"That's because he's so ugly," said Leslie.

"I'm sure he's quite handsome," said Mrs. Jewls. "He's just shy. Here, let me help you." Mrs. Jewls took off Sammy's coat for him. But underneath it was still another raincoat, even dirtier and smellier than the first one.

They still couldn't see his face.

"Ooooh, now he smells even worse," said Maurecia.

"You don't exactly smell like a rose, either," Sammy replied.

Mrs. Jewls took off his second raincoat, but there was still another one under that. And the smell became so bad that Mrs. Jewls had to run and stick her head out the window to get some fresh air.

"You're all a bunch of pigs!" Sammy screeched. "Dirty, rotten pigs!"

The smell was overpowering. Sammy just stood there, hidden under his raincoats.

Mrs. Jewls wrote Sammy's name under the word DISCIPLINE.

"Send him home on the kindergarten bus," said Joy.

"Not with me," said Todd.

Mrs. Jewls held her nose, walked up to Sammy, and removed his raincoat. She threw it out the window. But he had on still another one.

Sammy hissed. "Hey, old windbag, watch where you throw my good clothes!"

Mrs. Jewls put a check next to Sammy's name on the blackboard. Then she took off another raincoat and threw it out the window. The smell got worse, for he had on still another one.

Sammy began to laugh. His horrible laugh was even worse than his horrible voice.

When Sammy first came into the room, he was four feet tall. But after Mrs. Jewls removed six of his raincoats, he was only three feet tall. And there were still more raincoats to go.

Mrs. Jewls circled his name and removed another coat. She threw it out the window. Then she put a triangle around the circle and threw another one of his coats outside. She kept doing this until Sammy was only one-and-a-half feet high. With every coat she took off, Sammy's laugh got louder and the smell got worse.

Some of the children held their ears. Others could hold only one ear because they were holding their nose with the other hand. It was hard to say which was worse, the laugh or the smell.

Sammy stopped laughing and said, "Hey, old windbag, if you take off one more of my coats and throw it out the window, I'll bite your head off."

"They smell too bad for me to allow them in my classroom," said Mrs. Jewls. "You can pick them up when you leave."

"They smell better than you do, Pighead!" Sammy shouted.

Mrs. Jewls didn't stop. She took off another one of his coats, then another, and another. Sammy was only four inches tall, three inches tall, two inches tall. At last she removed the final coat.

All that was there was a dead rat.

"Well, I don't allow dead rats in my classroom," said Mrs. Jewls. She picked it up by the tail, put it in a plastic bag, and threw it away.

Mrs. Jewls didn't allow dead rats in her class. Todd once brought in a dead rat for show-and-tell, and Mrs. Jewls made him throw that one away, too.

"I'm glad Sammy isn't allowed in our classroom," said Rondi. "I didn't like him very much."

"Yes," said Mrs. Jewls, "we caught another one."

Dead rats were always trying to sneak into Mrs. Jewls's class. That was the third one she'd caught since September.

15
DEEDEE

This story contains a problem and a solution.

Deedee was a mousey looking kid. Unlike most children at Wayside School, she liked recess better than spelling. As soon as the recess bell rang, she would jump up from her seat and run out the door.

There were big signs in Wayside School on every floor, "NO JUMPING DOWN THE STAIRS."

Deedee never seemed to notice the signs. She jumped down the stairs. Some children took the stairs two at a time. Deedee took them ten at a time. That was on the way down. It was funny. She never seemed to be in quite the same hurry on the way back up.

There was another sign at Wayside School, "NO CUTTING ACROSS THE GRASS." Deedee must not ever have seen that one, either. She cut across the grass and ran up to Louis, the yard teacher.

"I want a green ball," Deedee said. The green balls were the best.

"I'm all out of green balls," said Louis.

"Okay, then I want a red ball," said Deedee. The red balls were just about as good as the green balls. They didn't bounce as high, but actually, sometimes you don't want a ball to bounce too high.

"I'm all out of red balls, too," said Louis.

"Do you have anything left?" asked Deedee.

Deedee meant anything besides the yellow ball. There was one yellow ball at Wayside School and Louis was always trying to get rid of it. It didn't bounce, and it never went the way it was kicked.

"Anything at all?" asked Deedee.

"Today is your lucky day," said Louis. "I have one ball left, just for you; the one and only yellow ball!"

"No, thanks," said Deedee.

"Aw, come on, take it," said Louis.

"Why don't you ever have any green or red balls?" asked Deedee.

"I do," said Louis. "But the other children ask first. By the time you get out here, they're all gone."

"But that's because I have to come all the way from the thirtieth story. How do you expect me to compete with the kids from the first or second?" she asked.

"That's why I saved you the yellow ball," said Louis. "Everybody wanted it, but I saved it just for you."

"I bet," said Deedee.

She took the yellow ball and bounced it on the ground. It stopped dead with a thud. She stepped back, ran up, and kicked it. It went backwards over her head. She didn't bother chasing it.

Instead she played hopscotch with Jennie and Leslie. She thought it was disgusting.

The next day, Deedee asked Mrs. Jewls if she could go to recess early.

"Why?" asked Mrs. Jewls.

"So I can get a green ball before Louis gives them all away," said Deedee.

"I'm glad you have a good reason," said Mrs. Jewls. "Yes, you may go. But first, spell *Mississippi* for me."

Spelling was not Deedee's best subject. By the time she finally got it right, she was five minutes late for recess.

She jumped down the stairs, cut across the grass, and ran up to Louis. There were no green balls left. There were no red balls left, either. However, there was still the yellow ball.

Deedee played jump rope with Joy and Maurecia. It was no better than hopscotch.

So Deedee's problem was to figure out a way to get a green ball, or at least a red ball.

You already know that this story also contains a solution. Deedee figured it out. See if you can, too. Remember every-thing you know about Deedee, Wayside School, and Mrs. Jewls.

Hint: The next day, Deedee brought a cream cheese and jelly sandwich, some nuts, and shredded cheese in her lunchbox.

Here's what happened.

Just before recess, Deedee smeared the cream cheese and jelly all over her face. Then she stuffed her mouth with nuts and hung the shredded cheese from her nose. When she closed her eyes, she looked just like a dead rat.

Todd was in on the plan. "Mrs. Jewls," he called. "There's a dead rat in the classroom."

Mrs. Jewls was very put out. "I want that dead rat outside immediately!"

When Mrs. Jewls said *immediately*, she meant it. Deedee instantly found herself outside on the playground.

"I want a green ball," she said.

Louis pretended that he hadn't heard her.

"May I *please* have a green ball?" asked Deedee.

Louis gave her a green ball. "I don't know how you did it, Deedee, but you're first today," he said.

When Mrs. Jewls found out that Deedee and Todd had tricked her, she sent Todd home early on the kindergarten bus.

Deedee threw the green ball on the ground. It bounced fifty feet straight up in the air, and then she caught it.

"You don't like me, do you?" she asked Louis.

"Sure I do," said Louis.

"No, you don't," said Deedee.

"Yes, I like you," said Louis.

"No, you don't," Deedee insisted.

113

"Yes, I like you. I really do," said Louis.

"Are you sure?" asked Deedee.

"Yes," said Louis. "Don't you believe me?"

"I guess so," said Deedee.

"Do you like me?" asked Louis.

"You bet," said Deedee. "You're my best friend!"

"Terrific," said Louis. "I always wanted to be best friends with a dead rat."

16
D.J.

D.J. skipped up the thirty flights of stairs to Mrs. Jewls's room. He was grinning from ear to ear, from nose to chin, from here to there, and back again.

"Hey, D.J.," Todd shouted, "glad to see you." Todd was a pushover for smiling faces.

Mrs. Jewls heard him. She began to write Todd's name on the board under DISCIPLINE, but when she saw D.J.'s smile, she put down the chalk. "Good morning, D.J.," she said. "What are you so happy about?"

D.J. grinned and shrugged his shoulders.

Mrs. Jewls smiled.

Dameon looked at the smile on Mrs. Jewls's face, then at Todd's, and finally at D.J.'s. Then Dameon smiled, too. His smile was almost as big as D.J.'s. They were best friends.

Once they saw the two of them smiling, the rest of the class couldn't help but smile. Rondi had a very cute one, due to her two missing front teeth. Nobody had an ugly smile.

Jason came to school late. He was very upset. But the first thing he saw was

Dameon's smile, and he felt a little bit better. Then he saw Rondi's toothless grin, and he even began to smile a little himself. But when he saw the piano on D.J.'s face, he fell, laughing, onto the floor.

Everybody started to laugh, even Kathy, and she hardly ever laughed except when someone hurt himself.

The whole room seemed to be laughing, not just the people in it. The blackboard chuckled. The ceiling snickered. The desks were jumping up and down, and the chairs were slapping one another on the back. The floor was very ticklish. It laughed until the walls turned purple. The wastepaper basket started to sing, and all the pencils stood up and danced.

Finally things began to settle down. Mrs. Jewls wiped her eyes and said, "D.J., why don't you tell the class why you are so happy? At least let us know what we are laughing about."

But D.J. just kept on smiling.

"Aw, come on, D.J.," said Deedee. "Tell us."

D.J. didn't say a word. He couldn't. His mouth was stretched out of shape.

"Let us guess," said Ron. "If we guess right, will you tell us?"

D.J. nodded his head. His smile began to hurt his ears.

Everyone took one guess.

"Have you been swimming?"

"Is it your birthday?"

"Are you in love?"

"Did you get a green ball?"

Nobody guessed right.

At recess D.J. was still smiling.

Louis, the yard teacher, called, "Hey, D.J. Come here."

They walked to the far corner of the playground, where they were alone.

"What's up, D.J.?" Louis asked.

D.J. just smiled.

"Come on, D.J. You can tell me. Why are you so happy?"

D.J. looked up at him. He said, "You need a reason to be sad. You don't need a reason to be happy."

17
JOHN

John had light brown hair and a round head. He was Joe's best friend. John was one of the smartest boys in Mrs. Jewls's class. But he had one problem. He could only read words written upside down.

Nobody ever wrote anything upside down.

But it was only a little problem. John was still in the high reading group. He just turned his book upside down.

It was easier for John to turn his book upside down than to learn to read correctly. But the easiest way isn't always the best way.

Mrs. Jewls said, "John, you can't go on reading like this. You can't spend the rest of your life turning your books upside down."

"Why not?" asked John.

"Because I said so," said Mrs. Jewls. "Besides, what happens when I write something on the blackboard? You can't turn the blackboard upside down."

"No, I guess you're right," said John.

"I know I'm right," said Mrs. Jewls. "You are going to have to learn to stand on your head."

John couldn't stand on his head. He had given up trying. You would have, too, if you had fallen over as many times as he had.

Joe was John's best friend. He could stand on John's head. Every time John fell over, Joe stood on his head. After all, what are best friends for?

"My head is too round, Mrs. Jewls. I can't stand on it," said John.

"Of course you can, John," said Mrs. Jewls. "If Joe can stand on your head, so can you."

"It's easy, John," said Joe.

"I can't," John repeated. "I always fall over."

"Nonsense," said Mrs. Jewls. "All you have to do is find your center of balance. Now, up you go."

John put his round head on the floor and swung his legs up. He fell right over. Then Joe stood on John's head.

"See, John, it's easy. Nothing to it," Joe said.

"We'll help you, John," said Mrs. Jewls. "Joe, get off John's head and get me the pillow from under my desk. Nancy, Calvin, come here and give us a hand."

Mrs. Jewls took the pillow from Joe and set it on the floor. "All right, John, we'll surround you," she said. "We won't let you fall."

John put his head on the pillow and swung his legs up. He started to fall one way, but Nancy pushed him back up. Then he started to fall another way, but Calvin straightened him out. John kept falling a little bit this way and that way until at last he found his center of balance.

"Hey, look at me. Look at me," said John. "I'm up. I'm really up. I'm standing on my head. I found my center of balance. It's beautiful. I can read the blackboard! Hey, Calvin, bring me a book, and you don't have to turn it upside down. Ha Ha. Hey, who, aaaaahhhh...."

BAMM!! While Calvin went to get the book, John fell flat on his face.

"You better stay off my head, Joe," he warned.

"Are you all right, John?" asked Mrs. Jewls.

"Yes, I think so. I feel a little funny. Hey! I can still read the blackboard, and I'm not upside down. I can read right side up now. When I fell, I must have flipped my brain or something."

"That is wonderful, John," said Mrs. Jewls. "Here, put the pillow back under my desk. As a reward you may have a Tootsie Roll pop. They are in the coffee can on top of my desk."

John placed the pillow on top of her desk. Then he looked under the desk, but he couldn't find the Tootsie Roll pops anywhere.

18
LESLIE

Leslie had five fingers on each hand and five toes on each foot. For each hand she had an arm, and for each foot she had a leg. She was a very lucky girl. And she had two lovely, long brown pigtails that reached all the way down to her waist.

When Mrs. Jewls asked a question, Leslie could raise one of her hands.

When Leslie was adding, she could count on her fingers.

When Paul pulled one of her pigtails, she could kick him with one foot while standing on the other.

But Leslie had one problem. She didn't know what to do with her toes. She had ten adorable little toes and nothing to do with them. As far as she could tell, they served no useful purpose.

"Suck your toes. That's what I do," said Sharie.

But Leslie's foot wouldn't reach her mouth.

"Well, that's all toes are good for," said Sharie. She put her foot in her mouth and went to sleep.

"No," thought Leslie. "They must be good for something. They just have to be."

During recess, she asked Dana. "Dana, what do you do with your toes?"

"I scratch the back of my legs," said Dana. "First I scratch my left leg with my right foot. Then I scratch my right leg with my left foot."

"But my legs don't itch," said Leslie.

"That's good," said Dana. "In that case you can scratch my legs. With your help I can scratch both legs at the same time."

"No, never mind," said Leslie. She walked up behind Louis, the yard teacher, and hopped on his shoulders.

"Louis," said Leslie. "I don't know what to do with my toes."

Louis tugged her foot. "Yes, that is a serious problem," he said, "but I'll tell you what I'll do. I'll take them off your hands for you, or rather, your feet. Just cut them off and give them to me."

"What?" asked Leslie.

"You don't want them, so I'll take them," said Louis. "You won't have to worry about them ever again."

"No," said Leslie.

"I'll give them to Miss Mush," said Louis. "She can make little hot dogs out of them." Miss Mush was the lunch teacher.

"No, I'm not going to give my toes away," said Leslie.

"All right," said Louis. "I'll give you a nickel apiece for them."

"No, you can't have them," said Leslie.

"Why not?" Louis asked. "They're no good to you, anyhow. And think of all you can buy for fifty cents."

The bell rang.

"I'll think it over," said Leslie. She ran back to class.

"Mrs. Jewls," said Leslie, "I don't see any reason for keeping my toes."

"Oh, Leslie, I'm sure there are lots of good reasons," said Mrs. Jewls.

"Well, I can't think of any. My legs don't itch, and I can't get my foot in my mouth. Louis offered me a nickel apiece for them, and it seems to me like a good deal. But I wanted to check with you first."

"I think Louis was pulling your leg," said Mrs. Jewls.

"No," said Leslie, "he was pulling my toes."

"What would he want with your toes?" asked Mrs. Jewls.

"I don't know," said Leslie, "but if he's willing to give me five cents apiece for them, then I'm going to take him up on it. That's fifty cents."

At lunch, Leslie walked up to Louis. "Okay, Louis," she said, "you can have my toes for a nickel apiece. That will be fifty cents."

"Not so fast," said Louis. "Let me look at them first."

Leslie took off her shoes.

"Yes, yes," said Louis, "the big ones are good, and the ones next to them, but the most I'll give you for the rest of your toes is three cents each."

Leslie was furious. "Three cents each! You told me five at recess."

"I'll give you five cents for the big ones. But just look at that scrawny little runt of a toe on the end, there. You're lucky to be getting even three cents for it. I think you're getting a darn good deal."

"I happen to like that toe," said Leslie.

"Fine, then," said Louis, "keep it. I'll just take the two big toes, and we'll call it square." He reached in his pocket and pulled out a dime.

"Nothing doing," said Leslie. "These toes are sold as a set. It's either all ten for fifty cents or no deal. What am I going to do with just eight toes?"

"Then forget it," said Louis. "I'm not going to give you a nickel for those scrawny little end toes."

"Fine," said Leslie, "no deal. My toes will still be here if you change your mind." She turned and walked toward the hopscotch area.

"Wait a second," Louis called. "I'll give you a dollar each for your pigtails."

Leslie turned around and looked at him with fiery eyes. "Cut my hair!" she exclaimed. "Are you crazy?"

19
MISS ZARVES

There is no Miss Zarves. There is no nineteenth story. Sorry.

20
KATHY

Kathy doesn't like you. She doesn't know you, but she still doesn't like you. She thinks you are stupid! In fact, she thinks you are the stupidest person she doesn't know. What do you think of that?

She also thinks you're ugly! As a matter of fact, she thinks you are the ugliest person she doesn't know. And she doesn't know a lot of people.

She doesn't like the people she knows, either. She hates everybody in Mrs. Jewls's class. She did like one member of the class. She liked Sammy. She thought he was funny. Sammy was a dead rat.

But Kathy has good reasons for not liking any of the children she knows. She doesn't like D.J. because he smiles too much, and she doesn't like John because he can't stand on his head.

Kathy once had a cat named Skunks. She liked Skunks. But she was afraid that Skunks would run away.

"You have nothing to worry about, Kathy," said Mrs. Jewls. "Skunks won't run away. Just be nice to him and feed him and pet him, and he won't run away. He may go out and play, but he'll always come back."

"No, you're wrong, Mrs. Jewls," said Kathy. "What do you know! He'll run away."

So Kathy kept Skunks locked up in her closet at home. She never let him out and sometimes even forgot to feed him.

One day, while Kathy was looking for her other shoe, Skunks ran out of the closet and never came back.

"You said he would come back, Mrs. Jewls," said Kathy. "He never came back. You were wrong. I was right."

That was why Kathy didn't like Mrs. Jewls.

"The next time I get a cat, I'll kill him. Then he'll never run away," said Kathy.

Then there was the time that Dameon tried to teach Kathy how to play catch.

Dameon said, "When I throw you the ball, Kathy, try to catch it."

"I can't catch it," said Kathy. "I'll just get hurt."

"You won't get hurt," Dameon insisted. "Just watch the ball."

He tossed it to her.

But Kathy knew she'd get hurt. So she closed her eyes. The ball hit her on the cheek. It hurt.

Kathy began to cry. "You were wrong," she sobbed. "I was right!"

That was why Kathy didn't like Dameon.

Allison believed that if you are nice to someone, then they'll be nice to you. So one day she brought Kathy a cookie.

"I don't want your ugly cookie," said Kathy. "It probably tastes terrible!"

Allison said, "No, it is very good. I made it myself."

Kathy said, "If you made it, then it must stink! You can't cook. You're too stupid!"

She just put the cookie in her desk along with her pencils, crayons, and books.

Three weeks later, Kathy was hungry. "All right, Allison," she said. "I'll try your stupid cookie." She took it out of her desk. It was covered with dust. She bit it. It was hard and tasted terrible.

"See," said Kathy. "I was right!"

That was why Kathy didn't like Allison.

Yes, Kathy had very good reasons for not liking anybody she knew.

But she also has a good reason for not liking you. And she doesn't even know you. Her reason is this. She knows that if you ever met her, you wouldn't like her. You don't like Kathy, do you?

See, she was right!

It's funny how a person can be right all the time and still be wrong.

21
RON

Ron had curly hair and little feet. "I want to play kickball," he said.

"You can't play," said Terrence.

"Get out of here," said Deedee.

"Scram," said Jason.

"I want to play kickball," said Ron.

"Well, you're not playing," said Terrence. "Beat it!" Ron stomped across the playground to the hopscotch area. Jenny was playing hopscotch with Louis. Jenny was on nine. Louis was still on four, but it was his turn.

"I want to play kickball," Ron said.

"So, go play kickball," said Louis.

"Terrence won't let me play," said Ron.

Louis walked with Ron to the kickball field.

"Hey, what about our hopscotch game?" Jenny asked.

"You won," said Louis.

"I just beat Louis in hopscotch!" Jenny announced. Leslie, Rondi, and Allison flocked around her.

"Hey, Louis," Dameon shouted. "Do you want to play kickball?"

"All right," said Louis. "Ron and I will both play."

"No," said Terrence. "Ron isn't playing."

"Anyone who wants to play can play," said Louis.

"No, he can't," said Terrence. "It's my ball."

"It isn't your ball," said Louis.

"You gave it to me," said Terrence.

"I gave it to you to share," said Louis. "If you can't share it, you can't have it."

"Oh, all right," said Terrence. "But I get to pitch."

"Ron and I will stand everybody!" Louis announced.

"All right!" said Jason. "We'll kill them!"

"We'll murder them!" said Deedee.

"We'll smash them!" said Myron.

"We'll see," said Louis.

Ron pitched, and Louis played the other eight positions. Twenty minutes later, they finally got three outs. The score was twenty-one to nothing.

Ron was up first.

"Infield in!" shouted Dameon. Everybody stood within ten feet of home plate.

"All right, Ron," Louis shouted, "kick it over their heads!"

Ron kicked the ball only three-and-a-half feet. Todd picked it up and threw him out.

Louis was up. Everybody ran back to the edge of the outfield. Still, Louis kicked the ball over their heads for a home run.

Everybody ran all the way back in again for Ron's up. He kicked the ball only two feet. Deedee tagged him out.

Louis kicked another home run.

Ron then kicked the ball a foot and tripped over it on his way to first base. Three outs.

Ron and Louis held the other team to only five runs the next inning. That was because the bell rang. Lunch was finally over.

Louis and Ron lost twenty-six to two. Ron had had a wonderful time.

The next day Ron said, "I want to play kickball."

"You can't play," said Terrence.

"Get out of here," said Jason.

"Scram," said Deedee.

"I want to play kickball," Ron told Louis.

Louis walked with him to the kickball field. "Ron and I will stand all of you."

Everybody liked the teams.

Ron pitched while Louis played the other eight positions. They lost fifty-seven to two.

After the game Louis took Ron aside. "Listen. Ron," he said, "why do you always want to play kickball? You can't kick. You can't field. You can't even run to first base. You just get smashed every game."

"Hey, now wait a second," said Ron. "Don't go blaming it all on me. You're half the team, too, you know." And with that, he punched Louis in the stomach.

And he punched a heck of a lot harder than he kicked.

22
The Three Erics

In Mrs. Jewls's class there were three children named Eric: Eric Fry, Eric Bacon, and Eric Ovens. They were known throughout the school for being fat. Eric Fry sat at this end of the room. Eric Bacon sat in the middle of the room. And Eric Ovens sat at that end of the room. There was a joke around Wayside School that if all three Erics were ever at the same end of the room at the same time, the whole school would tip over.

Eric Bacon hated jokes like that. That's not surprising. After all, he wasn't even fat. In fact, he was the skinniest kid in Mrs. Jewls's class. But nobody seemed to notice. The other two Erics were fat, and so everyone just thought that all Erics were fat.

"But I'm not fat!" Eric Bacon insisted.

"What's your name?" asked Jason.

"Eric," said Eric Bacon.

"Then you're fat," Jason concluded.

And pretty soon, skinny little Eric Bacon, the skinniest kid in Mrs. Jewls's class, had the nickname "Fatso."

Eric Fry really *was* fat. He was also the best athlete in Mrs. Jewls's class. His body was solid muscle. However, nobody ever noticed.

The other two Erics weren't very good at sports. Eric Ovens was clumsy. Eric ("Fatso") Bacon was a good athlete for his size, but because he was so skinny he didn't have much power.

So, naturally, everybody just assumed that Eric Fry was also clumsy and weak. After all, his name *was* Eric.

Whenever the other kids chose up teams, Eric Fry was the last one picked. They never noticed his home runs or the fabulous catches he made. Like all great athletes, he made the impossible look easy. Of course, the other kids did notice the one time that he dropped the ball.

Eric Fry was playing right field. Terrence belted a deep fly to left. Eric Fry raced all the way across the field after the ball and at the last second dived at it. He caught it in midair on his fingertips, but as he hit the ground the ball squirted loose.

"Well, what do you expect from 'Butterfingers,'" said Stephen.

And since that time Eric Fry has had the nickname "Butterfingers."

Eric Ovens was the nicest person in Mrs. Jewls's class. He treated everyone equally and always had a kind word to say. But because his name was Eric, everyone thought he was mean.

"Fatso" was mean because everyone called him "Fatso."

"Butterfingers" was mean because he always had to play right field.

So, naturally, everyone just assumed that Eric Ovens was also mean. They called him "Crabapple."

"Good morning, Allison," said Eric Ovens. "How are you?"

"Lay off, 'Crabapple'! Will ya?" answered Allison. "If you don't have something nice to say, don't say anything at all."

All three of the Erics had nicknames. It was better that way. Otherwise when someone said, "Hey, Eric," no one knew to whom he was talking. One time all the Erics would answer, and the next time none of them would answer. But when someone said, "Hey, 'Crabapple,'" then Eric Ovens knew they were talking to him. And if someone said, "Hey, 'Butterfingers,'" Eric Fry knew they meant him. And when someone said, "Hey, 'Fatso,'" Eric Bacon knew that he was being called.

23
ALLISON

Allison had pretty blonde hair and always wore a sky-blue windbreaker. Her windbreaker was the same color as her eyes. She was best friends with Rondi. Rondi had blonde hair, too, but she was missing her two front teeth. Allison had all of her teeth.

Allison used to say that she knocked Rondi's teeth out. Allison was very pretty, so all the boys in Mrs. Jewls's class teased her, especially Jason. But Allison said, "Leave me alone or I'll knock your teeth out — like I did Rondi's." The boys didn't bother her after that.

One day Allison brought a tangerine for lunch. She took the peel off in one piece.

Miss Mush, the lunch teacher, walked up to her. "Allison, may I have your tangerine?" she asked.

Miss Mush always gave food to the children. So Allison was happy to give her tangerine to Miss Mush.

Miss Mush shoved it in her mouth and swallowed it in less than four seconds.

Allison left the lunchroom and walked down to the library. The lunchroom was on the fifteenth story. The library was on the seventh. Allison already had her book. She just went to the library because it was nice and quiet there.

The librarian walked up to Allison. "What are you reading?" she asked.

Allison told her the name of the book.

"That sounds like a good book," said the librarian. "I never read that one. May I borrow it?"

The librarian always lent books to the children. Allison was glad to be able to return the favor. She gave the librarian the book, then walked down the stairs, outside to the playground.

All of Allison's friends were playing freeze tag. Allison didn't feel like playing. She reached into the pocket of her sky-blue windbreaker and took out a tennis ball. She bounced it a couple of times on the ground.

Louis came up to her. "Hi, Allison," he said. "May I play with your tennis ball?"

Louis always gave balls to the children. Allison happily gave her ball to Louis.

Louis threw the ball all the way to the other side of the playground. Then he went chasing after it.

Allison didn't feel like doing anything. Jason ran up and tagged her.

"You're frozen," he said.

"Get out of here before I knock your teeth out," said Allison.

Jason shrugged his shoulders and left.

Allison went back inside and up the thirty flights of stairs to Mrs. Jewls's room. The lunch period wasn't over yet, but Allison didn't feel like doing anything else. She had given her food to the lunch teacher, her book to the librarian, and her ball to the yard teacher. She went inside her classroom.

Mrs. Jewls was there. "Oh, Allison, I'm glad you're here," said Mrs. Jewls. "I'm having trouble with an arithmetic problem. Maybe you can help."

"Sure," said Allison. Mrs. Jewls always helped the children with their problems. Allison was happy to help.

"How do you spell *chair*?" asked Mrs. Jewls.

"C-H-A-I-R," said Allison.

"Yes, that's right," said Mrs. Jewls. "I knew it wasn't C-H-A-R-E, but I couldn't remember what it was."

"That's not an arithmetic problem," said Allison. "That's spelling."

"Yes, you are right again," said Mrs. Jewls. "I always get the two mixed up."

The bell rang. The lunch period was over. Allison could hear the other children running up the stairs.

"Allison," said Mrs. Jewls. "You learned a very important secret today, and I don't want you to tell any of the other children, not even Rondi."

"What was that?" asked Allison. She didn't even know she had learned a secret. She loved secrets.

"You learned that children are really smarter than their teachers," said Mrs. Jewls.

"Oh, that's no secret," said Allison. "Everybody knows that."

24
DAMEON

Dameon had hazel eyes with a little black dot in the middle of each of them. The dots were called pupils. So was Dameon. He was a pupil in Mrs. Jewls's class.

Mrs. Jewls was about to show the class a movie. She turned out the lights. When it was dark, Dameon's pupils got bigger.

"Dameon," said Mrs. Jewls, "run downstairs and ask Louis if he'd like to see the movie with us."

Dameon ran down the thirty flights of stairs to the playground. He stepped outside as Louis was hooking up a tetherball.

"Hey, Louis," Dameon called. "Do you want to see a movie in Mrs. Jewls's class?"

Louis rubbed his chin. "What movie?" he asked.

Dameon shrugged his shoulders. "I don't know," he said. "I'll be right back."

Dameon ran all the way back up the stairs to the thirtieth story.

"Louis wants to know, what movie?" said Dameon.

"Does he want to know the name of the movie or what the movie is about?" asked Mrs. Jewls.

"I don't know, said Dameon. "I'll ask him."

Dameon raced back down the stairs and out to the playground.

"Louis, do you want to know the name of the movie or what the movie is about?" he asked.

"The name," said Louis.

"Okay," said Dameon.

Dameon hurried back up the thirty flights of stairs. He took the steps two at a time.

"He wants to know the name," said Dameon.

"*Turtles*," said Mrs. Jewls.

Dameon turned around, took a deep breath, then ran back down the stairs.

"*Turtles*," Dameon told Louis.

"Hey, that might be good," said Louis. "What's it about?"

"I'm not sure," said Dameon. "I'll find out."

Dameon raced back up the stairs. But first he stopped to take a drink of water.

"What's it about, Mrs. Jewls?" asked Dameon.

"Turtles," said Mrs. Jewls.

Dameon rushed back down the stairs to tell Louis.

"Turtles," said Dameon.

"No, thanks," said Louis. "I don't like turtles. They are too slow."

Dameon lowered his head and slowly walked up the thirty flights of stairs. His legs were sore, he could hardly breathe, and his side ached.

By the time he got to Mrs. Jewls's class, the movie was over.

"All right, class," said Mrs. Jewls. "I want everybody to take out a piece of paper and a pencil and write something about turtles."

Dameon had missed the movie, but he still could have written something about turtles: "Turtles are too slow." But now he couldn't find his pencil. It just wasn't his day.

"What's the matter, Dameon?" asked Mrs. Jewls.

"I can't find my pencil," said Dameon.

"Class, Dameon's pencil is missing," Mrs. Jewls announced. "What did it look like, Dameon?" she asked.

"It was long and yellow," said Dameon. "It had a black point at one end and a red eraser at the other."

"I found it," said Todd, "here, by the blackboard."

"Yes, that's it," said Dameon.

"No, there it is, in the corner by the waste basket," said "Crabapple."

"Hmmm, maybe that's it," said Dameon.

"Here it is," said John. "It's been in my desk the whole time."

"No, here it is in my hand," said Joe.

"I found it," said Rondi.

"Here it is," said Allison.

"I have it," laughed D.J.

"I found it," said Myron.

"Which one is yours, Dameon?" asked Mrs. Jewls.

Dameon studied each pencil. "They all look like mine," he said.

Fortunately, at that moment, Louis walked into the classroom. He handed Dameon a pencil.

"You dropped this when you were telling me about the movie," said Louis.

"Thanks," said Dameon.

"Okay, class," said Mrs. Jewls. "So that we have no more mix-ups, I want everybody to write his name on his pencil."

Dameon spent the rest of the day trying to write his name on his pencil.

Dameon's pencil couldn't write on itself. It was just like his beautiful hazel eyes with the black dots in the middle. They could see everything except themselves.

25
JENNY

Jenny came to school on the back of her father's motorcycle. She was late. Wayside School began at nine o'clock. It was almost nine-thirty. She kissed her father good-bye and raced up the thirty flights of stairs to Mrs. Jewls's room.

"I'm sorry I'm late, Mrs. Jewls, but my father's motorcycle lost a . . ." There was nobody there. The room was empty.

"Hello, hello," she cried. "Mrs. Jewls, Dana, Todd, anyone?"

There was no one in the room.

"Maybe I'm early," Jenny thought. She looked up at the clock. It was exactly nine-thirty.

"Oh, I hope they didn't go on a field trip without me." She looked out the window. Nobody was there, not even Louis.

Jenny didn't know what to do. She sat down at her desk. She watched the second hand go around on the clock. "I might as well catch up on my spelling," she thought. She opened her desk and took out her speller.

M-U-D spells *mud.*

"Where is everybody?"

B-L-O-O-D spells *blood*.

"I hope nothing happened to them."

B-L-A-C-K spells *black*.

Jenny heard footsteps coming down the hall. She began to work very fast.

H-A-C-K spells *hack*. S-M-A-C-K spells *smack*. Someone opened the door. Jenny turned around. "Ack!" she gasped.

He was a man Jenny had never seen before. He had a black mustache and a matching attaché case.

Jenny jumped out of her seat.

"Get back in your seat," the man said.

Jenny slowly sat down.

The man walked over and sat down in Dana's seat, facing Jenny. He opened his attaché case and removed some papers.

"What is your name?" he asked her.

"Jenny," Jenny whispered.

"Jenny?" the man repeated as if he didn't believe her.

"Well, it is actually Jennifer, Jenny for short," said Jenny.

"I see," said the man. He took the speller from Jenny's desk. Jenny's name was written across the top. He put the speller in his attaché case.

"What are you doing here, Jennifer?" he asked.

"This is my classroom," said Jenny.

"Are you sure?" the man asked.

"Yes, I think so. I mean —"

"Where is the rest of your class?" the man asked.

"I don't know," said Jenny, "maybe they went on a field trip."

"No," said the man. "They didn't go on a field trip."

"Well, I don't know where they are!" Jenny cried. "I was half an hour late today, and when I got here everybody was gone. Really! Did something happen to them?"

The man didn't answer her. He wrote something on a piece of paper. "Tell me something, Jennifer. When you came to school today and saw that nobody was here, weren't you somewhat puzzled?"

"Yes. Yes," said Jenny. "What happened to them?"

"If you are really so concerned and so puzzled," said the man, "why did you work on spelling?"

"I don't know," said Jenny.

"It would seem to me," the man said, "that if a child came to school and nobody was there, she might play games, or walk around, or go home, but certainly not work on spelling."

Jenny started to cry. "I didn't know what to do. I was late and had to ride on a motorcycle and nobody was here and now you are asking me all kinds of questions and I'm afraid of what has happened to Dana and Mrs. Jewls and Rondi and Allison."

The man didn't understand a word she said.

Jenny heard more footsteps. The man got up and opened the door. Two more men came in. One had a black mustache like the first man. The other man was bald.

Jenny was frightened by them.

"Does she know?" asked the newcomer with the mustache.

"She claims she knows nothing," the first man answered. "She says she was late today, and when she got here everybody was gone."

"Do you believe her?" asked the man with the bald head.

"I'm not sure. She was working on her speller when I walked in." He reached into his attaché case and took out Jenny's speller. He handed it to the man with the bald head.

The bald man read Jenny's name across the top of it. "Tell me, Jenny," he said, "why are you the only one here?"

"I don't know," said Jenny.

"Has this ever happened before?" he asked.

"No, never," said Jenny.

He gave Jenny her speller. "Put this inside your desk."

Jenny put it away.

"I'm satisfied," said the man with the bald head.

"Okay, Jennifer," said the first man, "you may go now."

Jenny got out of her seat.

"Jenny," the bald man called.

Jenny turned slowly around. "Yes?" she whispered.

"Next time, don't come to school on a Saturday."

26
TERRENCE

Terrence was a good athlete but a bad sport.

Rondi and Allison were playing two-square with a red ball.

"Can I play?" asked Terrence.

"No," Allison replied.

"You have to let me play," Terrence said. "Louis says we have to share the balls."

"Well, we're not sharing with you," said Allison.

"Oh, let him play," said Rondi.

"All right," said Allison. "We'll play three-square. You better play right."

"I will," said Terrence.

Allison bounced the ball to Rondi. Rondi bounced it over to Terrence. Terrence caught it and kicked it over the fence.

"You have to go get it," said Allison.

"Shut up, Dixie cup," Terrence answered.

Rondi ran and told Louis.

D.J. and Dameon were playing basketball. "Uh-oh, here comes Terrence," said Dameon.

"Hey, let me play," said Terrence.

"Get lost, Terrence," said Dameon.

"You have to share the balls. Louis says so," said Terrence.

"Okay, but just throw it in the basket. Don't kick it," said Dameon.

"I won't," said Terrence.

First Dameon took a shot. It bounced off the backboard and through the hoop.

Next D.J. took a shot. He threw it underhand, way up in the air. It came down through the hoop without touching the rim.

Then Terrence took a shot. He kicked it over the fence.

"You idiot," said Dameon.

"Take a train, peanut brain," Terrence answered.

D.J. went and told Louis.

Stephen, Calvin, Joe, John, and Leslie were playing spud. Stephen was IT. Everyone else had a number. Stephen had to throw the ball up in the air and call out a number. The person who had that number had to try to catch it.

"Can I play?" asked Terrence.

"No," said Calvin. "You'll just kick the ball over the fence."

"No," said Joe.

"No way," said John.

"No," said Leslie.

"Sure," said Stephen. "Newcomers are IT." He gave the ball to Terrence. "Just throw the ball up in the air and call out a number between one and five."

"Okay," said Terrence.

The children formed a circle around Terrence.

"A million," yelled Terrence as he kicked the ball over the fence.

"What did you do that for?" asked Stephen.

"Eat a frog, warthog," said Terrence.

Stephen ran and told Louis.

Terrence looked around. There was nothing to do. There were no balls left.

Louis walked up to him. He was followed by Allison, Rondi, Dameon, D.J., Stephen, Calvin, Joe, John, and Leslie.

"What's the matter, Terrence?" asked Louis.

"There are no balls," said Terrence. "Do you have a green ball?"

"No," said Louis. "All of my balls have mysteriously disappeared."

"Darn it," said Terrence. "There is nothing left to kick."

"Nothing left to kick?" asked Louis. "Oh, I don't know about that. What do you think, Rondi? Is there anything left to kick?"

Rondi thought a minute. Then she smiled. She was missing her two front teeth. "Yes, there is something left to kick," she said.

"Well, where is it?" asked Terrence.

"Let me check with Allison," said Louis. "Allison, is there anything left to kick?" He winked at her.

"There sure is," said Allison.

"What, what?" asked Terrence.

"How about you, Dameon?" asked Louis. "Can you think of anything?"

Dameon nodded his head yes.

"Well, what is it?" asked Terrence. He couldn't wait.

"D.J., we got anything around here to kick?" asked Louis.

D.J. smiled. "Yes, we do," he said.

"Give it to me. Give it to me," Terrence demanded.

"I don't know if I should," said Louis. "What do you think, Calvin? Should I give it to him?"

"I think you should," said Calvin.

"You heard Calvin," said Terrence. "Give it to me."

"Not so fast," said Louis. "Leslie, should I give it to him?"

"Oh, yes, I think he deserves it," said Leslie.

"Give it to me. Give it to me," Terrence repeated.

"Do you also think he deserves it, Joe?" asked Louis.

"Yes, I think so," said Joe.

"What about you, John?" asked Louis.

"Definitely give it to him," John answered.

"Come on. Come on," said Terrence. "Recess is almost over."

"We'll leave it up to Stephen," said Louis. "Whatever he says goes."

"Let him have it," said Stephen.

"You heard him, Louis," said Terrence. "Let me have it."

"Okay," said Louis.

He picked Terrence up and kicked him over the fence.

27
JOY

Joy had forgotten her lunch at home. It was lunchtime. She was hungry.

She didn't have a meal ticket. If she had had a meal ticket, she could have had a lunch from Miss Mush, the lunch teacher. She'd have to be terribly hungry to eat a lunch made by Miss Mush. Even an empty brown paper sack would taste better. But that's how hungry Joy was.

Dameon hadn't forgotten his lunch. He had brought a lovely turkey sandwich, a big piece of chocolate cake, and a crisp, red apple. All he needed was a glass of milk. He could get that from Miss Mush. Miss Mush didn't know how to ruin milk.

Dameon left his lunch on his desk and went to the end of the milk line.

Joy didn't waste any time. She reached into Dameon's sack and took out the apple. But then she spotted the turkey sandwich. She put back the apple, took the sandwich, and noticed the chocolate cake. She put back the sandwich and took out the cake.

But then Joy had second thoughts. She put back the cake. Then she grabbed Dameon's whole lunch.

First she ate the sandwich. It was in a Baggie. When she finished the sandwich, she placed the Baggie on Jason's desk.

Next she ate the chocolate cake. It was wrapped in wax paper. She put the wax paper on Allison's desk.

She ate the apple last. She placed the apple core on Deedee's desk.

Then she put the empty sack on Calvin's desk.

Dameon returned with his glass of milk. "Mrs. Jewls, my lunch is gone!" he called.

"I wonder where it could be," said Mrs. Jewls.

"Calvin took it," said Joy. "There's the empty sack on his desk."

"Good work, Joy," said Mrs. Jewls. "Calvin, I'm ashamed of you." She wrote

Calvin's name on the blackboard under the word DISCIPLINE.

"Look, the Baggie from Dameon's turkey sandwich is on Jason's desk!" Joy called.

"Very good, Joy," said Mrs. Jewls. "But how did you know that Dameon had a turkey sandwich?"

"I'm just smart," said Joy.

Mrs. Jewls wrote Jason's name on the blackboard under Calvin's.

"And there's the wax paper from the delicious chocolate cake on Allison's desk," Joy announced. Joy had chocolate all around her lips.

Allison stood firm. She looked into Mrs. Jewls's eyes. "I didn't eat his cake," she said.

"The evidence is there on your desk," said Mrs. Jewls. "Joy spotted it." She wrote Allison's name under Jason's.

"Dameon's apple core is on Deedee's desk," said Joy.

"Very good, Joy," said Mrs. Jewls. She wrote Deedee's name under Allison's.

"Dameon, I think you ought to thank Joy," said Mrs. Jewls. "She solved the mystery."

"Thank you, Joy," said Dameon.

Just then, Louis, the yard teacher, walked in. "I have your lunch, Joy," he said. "Your mother brought it. You left it at home."

"You mean you didn't have a lunch?" asked Mrs. Jewls. "You must be very hungry."

"No," said Joy, "not really. Since Dameon didn't get to eat, he can have it."

"Thanks a lot!" said Dameon. "You are the greatest!"

He ate Joy's lunch, an old bologna sandwich and a dried-up carrot.

"Joy, for being such a good detective, and for being so generous with your lunch, you may help yourself to a Tootsie Roll pop," said Mrs. Jewls. "They are in the coffee can on top of my desk."

Joy took one. Then, when Mrs. Jewls wasn't looking, she took another.

Calvin, Jason, Allison, and Deedee had their names on the blackboard under the word DISCIPLINE. But they were good the rest of the day, so at two o'clock Mrs. Jewls erased them.

They forgot all about the whole thing.

Dameon had a lousy lunch instead of a great lunch. But five minutes later it didn't make any difference. He couldn't taste it anymore, and he was full. He went outside to play basketball and forgot about the whole thing.

Joy had a great lunch and two Tootsie Roll pops. But five minutes later it didn't make any difference. She couldn't taste it anymore, and she was full. And at dinnertime she was hungry, just the same.

But a horrible thing happened. Joy couldn't forget about filching Dameon's lunch. And for the rest of the year, every turkey sandwich, piece of chocolate cake, apple, and Tootsie Roll pop tasted like Miss Mush's porridge.

28
NANCY

Nancy had big hands and big feet. He didn't like his name. He thought it was a girl's name.

None of the other children in Mrs. Jewls's class thought that Nancy's name was odd. They didn't think of it as a girl's name or as a boy's name. Nancy was just the name of the quiet kid with the big hands and feet who sat over there in the corner next to John.

Nancy was very quiet and shy. He was ashamed of his name. He had only one friend, a girl who went to class on the twenty-third story of Wayside School.

They were friends for a good reason. He didn't know her name, and she didn't know his. They just called each other "Hey, you," or just plain "You."

Nancy was afraid to ask his friend what her name was because then he might have to tell her his name. He never could figure out why she never asked. But he was happy just to leave well enough alone.

One morning, Nancy and his friend were late. When they got to the twenty-third story, his friend's teacher was waiting outside.

"Hurry up. You're late, Mac," said the teacher.

Nancy's friend turned red. She didn't move.

"Come on, Mac, shake a leg. Get the lead out," said the teacher.

"Your name is Mac!" said Nancy.

Mac was very pretty. She had red hair and freckles. She covered her face and ran into the room.

"My name is Nancy!" Nancy called after her.

Mac stepped back outside. "I was ashamed to tell you my name," she said.

"Me, too," said Nancy. "Nancy's a girl's name."

"Oh, I think it's cute," said Mac.

"I like the name Mac," said Nancy.

"Mac is a boy's name," said Mac.

"My mother has a rich aunt named Nancy," said Nancy. "That's why she gave me the name."

"My mother once had a dog named Mac," said Mac.

"Hey, do you want to trade?" Nancy asked.

"Can we?" asked Mac.

"I don't see why not," said Nancy.

"Okay," said Mac.

They both spun around one hundred times in opposite directions until they were so dizzy that they fell over. When they stood up, Mac was Nancy and Nancy was Mac.

They said good-bye. Then Mac raced up to Mrs. Jewls's room. He was no longer shy.

"Hi, everybody. My name's Mac," he announced. "I traded names." He held out his big hand.

Todd jumped up and shook it. "Hi, Mac," he said. "Glad to meet you."

"How you doin', Mac," said Ron.

"Howdy, Mac," said Terrence.

"Nice to see you, Mac," said Bebe.

"You traded names?" asked Jason. Jason didn't like his name, either.

"That's right, Jason, old boy," said Mac.

"Is that allowed?" asked Jason.

"Why not!" said Mac.

"Hey, anybody want to trade?" Jason called.

"I'll trade with you," said Terrence. He didn't like his name, either.

"Wait. I'll trade with you, Terrence," said Maurecia. Maurecia didn't like her name.

"No. He's trading with me," said Jason.

"I'll trade with you, Maurecia," said Dameon.

189

"No, thanks," said Maurecia.

"I'll trade with you, Dameon," said Mrs. Jewls.

"No, I want to be Mrs. Jewls," said Stephen.

It turned out that nobody in Mrs. Jewls's class liked his name. The children all spun around in different directions until they got so dizzy that they fell over. And when they stood up again, nobody knew who anybody was.

"What are we going to do, Mrs. Jewls?" asked Leslie, who was really Eric Bacon.

"My name is not Mrs. Jewls. It's Maurecia," answered Terrence, who was really Jason.

"It is not. I'm Maurecia," said Deedee, who was really Joe.

"You're both wrong," said Maurecia. "I'm Mrs. Jewls."

This went on for an hour. At last they figured out who the real Rondi was. She was missing her two front teeth. After they figured out Rondi, they were able to get Allison pretty easily. And then from there they got D.J., Dameon, and Mrs. Jewls. She was the oldest one.

Eventually they figured out who everybody really was. They had some difficulty deciding which Eric was which, and actually they are still not absolutely sure.

Everybody just decided to keep his own name. The children didn't like them, but it made things much easier.

Mac and Nancy kept their new names. But when they were together they still called each other "Hey, you," or just plain "You."

29
STEPHEN

Stephen had green hair. He had purple ears and a blue face. He wore his sister's pink dancing shoes and green leotards. The leotards matched his hair. He was all dressed up as a goblin for Mrs. Jewls's Halloween party.

But unfortunately it wasn't Halloween.

"Ha, ha, ha, you sure look stupid," said Jason. Jason was Stephen's best friend.

"So do you," said Stephen.

"Boy, are you dumb," said Jenny. "Halloween is on Sunday. Today is only Friday."

"You're the one who's dumb," said Stephen. "Ha, ha, you'd probably come to school on Sunday. Mrs. Jewls said we'd have the party today."

But none of the other children wore costumes, only Stephen.

"All right, class," said Mrs. Jewls. "It is time for our Halloween party."

"See," said Stephen.

Mrs. Jewls gave each child a cookie that looked like an orange witch with a black hat. She laughed when she saw Stephen and forgot to give him one. Stephen didn't ask for it. He was afraid that she'd laugh again.

The children finished their cookies in less than thirty seconds.

"All right, class," said Mrs. Jewls. "The party is over. We have a lot of work to do."

Stephen felt like a fool. The party lasted less than a minute. And he had to spend the rest of the day wearing his stupid goblin suit.

"Look, Stephen's wearing his sister's leotards," laughed Dana.

"They're green, just like his hair," said "Fatso."

Everybody laughed.

Mrs. Jewls began the arithmetic lesson. She wrote on the blackboard. "Two plus two equals five."

"That's wrong!" Joy shouted.

Mrs. Jewls tried again. "Two plus two equals three."

194

That wasn't right, either. She added two and two again and got forty-three. It was useless. No matter how hard she tried, she could not get two plus two to equal four.

"I don't understand it," she said. "They've always equaled four before."

Suddenly she screamed. The chalk turned into a squiggling worm! She dropped it on her foot.

Then all the lights went out, and the blackboard lit up like a movie screen.

A woman appeared on the screen. She had a long tongue and pointed ears. She stepped off the screen and into the classroom.

It was the ghost of Mrs. Gorf.

Mrs. Gorf ran her fingernails across the blackboard. "Trick or treat, you rotten kids," she said. "Now I'll get even with every last one of you. Where's Todd?"

"Who is that?" asked Mrs. Jewls.

"Mrs. Gorf," said Dameon.

"Who's Mrs. Gorf?" asked Mrs. Jewls.

"She was the meanest teacher we ever had," said Rondi.

"What happened to her?" asked Mrs. Jewls.

"Louis ate her," said Jason.

"Well, I'm not going to allow this," said Mrs. Jewls. "Get out of my classroom!" she demanded.

"It's Halloween, sweet teacher," said Mrs. Gorf. "Ghosts can go anywhere they like. I've come for a little class reunion."

"But it isn't Halloween," said Mrs. Jewls. "Halloween is still two days away."

"I know," said Mrs. Gorf, "but Halloween falls on a Sunday this year, so we are celebrating it on the Friday before."

196

Stephen leaped up from his seat. "See, I was right," he said. "Today is the day we celebrate it, the Friday before! Mrs. Gorf proved it."

He ran up to Mrs. Gorf. "They all laughed at me and made me feel stupid because I was the only one who got dressed up. But they were the ones who were wrong. You and I are right."

He put his arms around Mrs. Gorf and hugged her.

Mrs. Gorf gasped and disappeared.

The lights came back on.

Mrs. Jewls picked up the piece of chalk from the floor. She wrote on the blackboard, "Two plus two equals four."

"That's good," she said. "When two plus two doesn't equal four, anything can happen."

All the children who had laughed at Stephen now called him a hero. But they told him to change out of his stupid costume.

So at lunch, Stephen went home, washed up, and changed. He came back wearing blue jeans and a polo shirt. Of course, his hair was still green. It always was.

30
LOUIS

Louis had a red face and a mustache of many colors. He was the yard teacher at Wayside School. It was his job to see that the children didn't have too much fun during lunch and recess.

And if you haven't already guessed, he is the one who wrote this book.

On June tenth there was a blizzard. Louis was afraid that the children would have too much fun, so nobody was allowed outside.

"Class," said Mrs. Jewls. "After you finish your lunch today, come back up to the classroom. You are not allowed outside."

The children all went to the lunchroom. Miss Mush had made Tuna Surprise. They looked at it, then hurried back up the stairs.

There was nothing to do.

"Now, class," said Mrs. Jewls, "I know that you are all bored, but I have a special surprise for you."

"I hope it's better than the Tuna Surprise," said Maurecia.

Mrs. Jewls continued, "Louis is going to come up and entertain us. He will tell us a story. Now I want you all to be on your best behavior."

When Louis walked in, all the children booed.

"Are you going to tell us a story?" asked Bebe.

"Yes," said Louis.

"Well, it better be good," Bebe warned.

"It better be better than the Tuna Surprise," said "Butterfingers."

"I thought the Tuna Surprise was good," said Louis.

"You'd eat dirt if they put enough ketchup on it," said Mac.

"Hey, everybody, be quiet," said Todd. "Let him tell the story."

"Not too loud, Louis," said Sharie. "I'm trying to get some sleep."

Louis sat in the middle of the room, and all the children gathered around.

Louis began his story. "This is a story about a school very much like this one.

But before we get started, there is something you ought to know so that you don't get confused. In this school every classroom is on the same story."

"Which one, the eighteenth?" asked Jenny.

"No, said Louis. "They are all on the ground. The school is only one story high."

"Not much of a school," laughed Dameon.

Louis continued. "Now you might think the children there are strange and silly. That is probably true. However, when I told them stories about you, they thought that you were strange and silly."

"US?" the children answered. "How are we strange?"

"I'm normal," said Stephen. "Aren't I?"

"As normal as I am," Joe assured him.

"The children at that school must be crazy," said Leslie.

"Real lulus," Maurecia agreed.

"Tell us about them, Louis," Bebe demanded.

"For one thing," Louis said, "none of these children has ever been turned into an apple."

"That's silly," said Deedee. "Everybody's been turned into an apple. It's part of growing up."

Louis continued. "Dead rats don't walk into classrooms wearing raincoats."

"What do they wear, tuxedos?" asked Todd.

"And girls never try to sell their toes," Louis added.

"Well, no wonder," said Leslie, "at today's prices."

Louis continued. "They don't trade names or read upside down. They can't turn mosquito bites into numbers. They don't count the hairs on their heads. The walls don't laugh, and two plus two always equals four."

"How horrible," said Dameon.

"That's not the worst of it," said Louis. "They have never tasted Maurecia-flavored ice cream."

A hush fell over the classroom.

"Mrs. Jewls, I'm scared," said Allison. "Is there really a school like that?"

"Of course not," said Mrs. Jewls. "Louis was just telling a story."

"It was a good story," said Leslie.

"I thought it was stupid," said Kathy.

"I liked it," said Rondi. "It was funny."

Mrs. Jewls said, "Louis, it was a very entertaining story. But we don't really go in for fairy tales here. I'm trying to teach my class the truth."

"That's all right," said Louis. "I have to go down to room twenty-nine now and tell them a story." He started out the door.

"Class," said Mrs. Jewls. "Let's all thank Louis for his wonderful story."

Everybody booed.

ABOUT THE AUTHOR

When **Louis Sachar** was going to school, his teachers always pronounced his name wrong. Now that he has become a popular author of children's books, teachers all over the country are pronouncing his name wrong. It should be pronounced "Sacker," like someone who tackles quarterbacks or someone who stuffs potatoes into sacks. Mr. Sachar's first book, *Sideways Stories from Wayside School*, was accepted for publication during his first year of law school. After receiving his law degree, he spent six years asking himself whether he wanted to be an author or a lawyer before deciding to write for children full-time. His books include *Sideways Stories from Wayside School*, *Wayside School Is Falling Down*, *Wayside School Gets a Little Stranger*, and *Holes*, winner of a Newbery Medal and National Book Award. He was born in East Meadow, New York, and now lives in Texas.

The employees of Thorndike Press hope you have enjoyed this Large Print book. All our Thorndike, Wheeler, and Kennebec Large Print titles are designed for easy reading, and all our books are made to last. Other Thorndike Press Large Print books are available at your library, through selected bookstores, or directly from us.

For information about titles, please call:
   (800) 223-1244

or visit our website at:
   http://gale.cengage.com/thorndike

To share your comments, please write:
   Publisher
   Thorndike Press
   10 Water St., Suite 310
   Waterville, ME 04901